PROTECTING THE BABY

JODIE BAILEY

Special thanks and acknowledgment are given to Jodie Bailey for her contribution to the Colorado K-9 Unit miniseries.

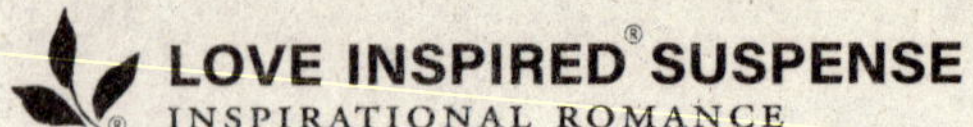

ISBN-13: 978-1-335-95781-8

Protecting the Baby

Love Inspired
22 Adelaide St. West, 41st Floor
Toronto, Ontario M5H 4E3, Canada
www.LoveInspired.com

HarperCollins Publishers
Macken House, 39/40 Mayor Street Upper,
Dublin 1, D01 C9W8, Ireland
www.HarperCollins.com

Printed in Lithuania

1 2 3 4 5 6 7 8 9 10 LIT 28 27 26 25

And God shall wipe away all tears from their eyes;
and there shall be no more death, neither sorrow,
nor crying, neither shall there be any more pain:
for the former things are passed away.
—*Revelation* 21:4

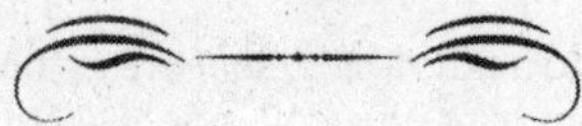

To my husband's family, who loved him into the amazing husband and father he is today.

ONE

One more gesture of goodwill…one more hug…or sympathetic look… One more *anything* and Carly Mayor might shatter.

She dropped her forehead to her Camry's steering wheel and prayed she'd open her eyes to the old normal. Her best friend would still be alive. Her life wouldn't be upside down. There wouldn't be a six-month-old babbling in the back seat.

And there wouldn't be a thousand people bombarding her with offers to help.

"I'm just saying, Carly. I can take Ariel for a couple of days and let you get some rest. A lot has happened quickly. You need time to grieve." The disembodied voice of Julia Crosby, the assistant district attorney of Oak City, Colorado, was coated in compassion.

It was enough to make Carly gag.

The offer to help wasn't the problem. In fact, it was appreciated.

The problem was the overwhelming truth that nothing would ever be the same again. Her best friend, Wendy, was gone. Wendy's husband, Mike, was gone. Carly's role had shifted from adoring godmother to full-time mom overnight.

She lifted her head and stared at the dark fog that had

drifted across the field into the trees that surrounded her small ranch-style home.

It was past sunset, and here on the outskirts of town, streetlights weren't a thing. Like her world, everything was dark. In her haste to get to the funeral, she'd forgotten to turn on any lights, so even her house appeared lifeless.

"Carly?" Julia's voice flooded the car again. "Do I need to come out there? Are you okay?"

"I'm fine." Carly straightened her spine. So many people were offering to help, but did they mean it? If life had taught her nothing else, it was that she could only count on herself…

She'd once thought that going into foster care at thirteen after her parents abandoned her in search of their next high had been the hardest thing she could endure.

She'd been wrong.

Exhaling loudly, she glanced in the rearview at the mirror that reflected Ariel in her rear-facing car seat. The baby was happily playing with her toes, oblivious to the chaos around her. "I'm fine, Julia, really. What I want right now is to go inside, get Ariel to sleep, then put my feet up. I promise I'll call if I need anything." She punched the *end* button on her steering wheel before Julia could respond.

It wasn't that she resented the help or didn't like Julia. When Wendy, Mike and Carly had all been in foster care in high school, Julia had been a friend to Mike's foster family. She was about ten years older and married to a local architect. Julia and her husband were kind and helpful, if a little pushy.

Right now, Carly just couldn't bear to part with Ariel, even for one night. The baby was all she had of Wendy and Mike after two horrific tragedies in the span of three weeks had left the infant orphaned and in Carly's care.

Wendy's funeral today had been a whirlwind, too close

on the heels of Mike's. Too many faces, too many sympathetic gestures, too many of everything. Images and sounds all blurred together. Her entire body ached, and she was glad she'd opted for Converse shoes with her dress instead of heels. She'd be a collapsed heap on the church floor by now if she'd chosen style over comfort.

It had been four days since Wendy had been killed in a car crash when she'd missed a curve and rolled down a ravine on a winding mountain road. Four days since Carly'd been handed custody of baby Ariel, who had been home with a babysitter while Wendy went to a job interview. Four days since Carly had taken a leave of absence from her job as a large-animal veterinarian at a practice she was poised to take over from Dr. Frank Tyndall within the next few years.

Four horrible, surreal days.

She had yet to cry. The pressure mounted in her chest and throat, but the tears refused to come. There was too much to do, too much concern for a little one who didn't understand why first her father and now her mother weren't comforting her in the middle of the night.

Ariel's babbling increased in intensity and demand.

Already, Carly knew that cry. She was hungry, and the world did not stop for a hungry baby.

Gathering what was left of her waning strength, Carly slipped out of the car and opened the back door, wishing that this borrowed car seat was the kind that Wendy had used, one that detached into a carrier. Instead, it was a fixed mount, requiring her to strap Ariel into a carrier on her chest if she wanted her hands free.

She unstrapped Ariel and had her fastened against her chest in no time. In the hot July night, the baby was a tiny heater as she snuggled in and whimpered.

"Just a few minutes, Jellybean." It had been Mike's nickname for his much-loved daughter, one that had been taken up by everyone who knew them. Carly hefted the backpack that held the household's worth of supplies it took to care for an infant and slung it onto her back, feeling like a pack mule. "Let's go."

She hip-checked the door shut and headed for the porch.

Headlights swept the front of the house, and gravel crunched as a pickup truck pulled into the driveway.

Carly slumped. She'd told the pastor not to bring food to the house tonight, that it could wait until tomorrow. Guess he, like everyone else, thought she'd forgotten how to survive on her own.

But when the truck door opened, it wasn't Pastor Gabe. Lit by the interior lights was a broad-shouldered bald man with a strong jaw and a scowl on his face. He was vaguely familiar, but she couldn't place him among the men of the church.

She instinctively wrapped one arm around Ariel as she backed toward the house and reached into her dress pocket for her keys. They were a good third of a mile through the woods from her nearest neighbor, and if this guy meant harm, she'd have to fight on her own.

He stopped to survey her, leaving the truck door open. The interior light was the only illumination in the dark yard. "You Carly Mayor?"

Honestly, she was done with this day. She pulled herself to her full height and hoped it made her seem intimidating, though that was doubtful with a baby strapped to her. "Who wants to know?"

"You've got Ariel Higgins?" His gaze drifted to the baby, his expression calculated. "I'm going to need you to turn her over to me."

Whoa. What? Carly pressed Ariel tighter to her chest, backing another step toward her porch, hoping she wasn't projecting fear. She gripped her keys like a weapon. Defending herself was second nature. "Again, who are you?"

He walked closer methodically, as though he was a lion on the prowl. He hefted a sheaf of papers she hadn't realized he was holding. "I'm her legal guardian per the will of Michael Higgins, and I'll be taking her with me."

A fierce sense of protectiveness over her precious goddaughter ran steel through her bones. It overwhelmed the fear she should probably be feeling.

Over her dead body would he take Ariel, although she certainly wouldn't say that out loud. This guy looked like the type who could make it happen. "I think you need to leave. If what you say is true, you can take it up with the courts, but I am not handing her to you." *Not now, not ever.* She was Ariel's family now. "Wendy's will was clear, as were her words nearly every single day of Ariel's life." Particularly in the weeks after Mike had died. It had almost become an obsession of Wendy's, constantly needing to hear that Carly would raise Ariel in a loving home if the unthinkable happened. "You need to leave. Now."

Gathering all her bravery, she stepped toward the man as though her five-foot-six self could somehow threaten over six feet of muscle.

He seemed to flinch, but in the moment it took that motion to register, he lunged, reaching for Ariel.

Carly skirted to the side, her steps hampered by the weight of the infant on her chest and the diaper bag on her back. The fear that had been dammed up somewhere inside her was unleashed, rushing forth in a roar.

This man would hurt her, would hurt Ariel, to get what he wanted.

She hesitated, torn between running for her house or her car. Which would get them to safety faster?

Her hesitation proved to be her undoing. The man whirled and grabbed her arm, reaching for the clip that held Ariel against her chest. "I'll take her now!"

He was going to grab the baby.

Not on her watch.

Reflexively, she swung her hand, her house key protruding from her fist, and hit the man in the side, hard.

He roared and released her as her keys clattered to the ground.

Carly stumbled, going down to one knee, fighting to stay upright lest she fall and injure Ariel, who wailed in terror.

Grasping a fistful of dirt, Carly scrambled to her feet. When the man approached again, she flung the loose soil into his face.

He clawed at his eyes, screaming obscenities, calling her names she'd hoped she'd never hear aimed in her direction again.

She didn't wait to hear more. There was no time to grab her keys. No way to get into her house or flee in her car. She'd been here before, hunted, nowhere to run…

She had to escape. She prayed she could outpace this man through the woods.

Cradling Ariel close and praying the baby wouldn't be hurt, she ran as fast as she dared, melting into the woods, hoping her attacker wouldn't be able to find her in the darkness…

Although Ariel's cries were a beacon in the night that would lead her attacker right to them.

It was one of those nights. The air was too heavy and still. He'd never sleep. The memories would dog him and the nightmares would chew him up and spit him out.

Oak City police officer Eli Blackwood stepped out onto

his back porch with his K-9 partner Wrangler at his heels. As he stared past the horse paddock and barn into the dark woods that ringed his property, the Belgian Malinois leaned the full weight of his sixty-plus-pound body against Eli's leg.

It was as though Wrangler understood the pain that coursed through Eli's veins with renewed vengeance tonight. No matter how much time passed or how many sleepless nights he endured, the grief never seemed to fully go away. It eased for stretches of time, but it always came back. Sometimes it was a needle's prick. Other times it was a knife to the heart.

He was almost relieved when grief crashed into him like a rogue wave. The moments when he seemed to forget made him feel guilty and negligent, as though memories of his wife and child were losing value.

They were the greatest treasures he'd ever known…and he'd lost them.

He'd failed them.

He let his hand fall to his side and scratched Wrangler behind the ears. Only his partner knew the fullness of Eli's grief. He certainly wasn't going to discuss it with anyone else. Three years later and it still burned, although he was certain many people in his life thought he should be "over it." How did one ever "get over" losing two thirds of his heart?

He dragged his hands down his face and leaned against the porch post by the brick steps, watching his two horses, Sandy and Thunder, wander to the far side of the paddock as they tried to catch an evening breeze. *Good luck with that.*

Today had been nothing but frustrating. The entire case he and Wrangler were working had been nothing but frustrating.

In fact, his whole team was suffering under the strain.

Three pregnant teenagers had been kidnapped and murdered, shot in the chest and their bodies dumped shortly after they'd given birth. Their infants were missing, presumably sold on the black market.

In response, the Colorado K-9 Unit had been formed, made up of various officers and agents from local, state and federal agencies, all working together to bring the illegal adoption ring to justice.

There was an added level of urgency, given that a fourth pregnant woman, nineteen-year-old Mia Andrews, had vanished three months earlier while dropping off food at her local food bank. The case hit close to home because her grandfather, Dodger Andrews, was a huge supporter of K-9 teams throughout Colorado. He was well known and well liked, and his grief and fear for his granddaughter and her unborn child were heartbreaking.

The case was eating Eli alive. Babies in danger. Mothers murdered.

It hit too close to home. He'd spent the past several months feeling sick to his stomach, wandering his house at night and wondering why he had ever joined the task force.

Why? Because he was the best investigative officer he could possibly be, and Wrangler was the most well-trained suspect apprehension and protection K-9 he'd ever partnered with. Those missing infants and their mothers deserved justice. Mia Andrews and her unborn child deserved to be rescued. There was no way he could sit on the sidelines and watch others do the work when he could help…

Even if his insides ate him alive.

Straightening, he turned to go into the house. He wasn't going to sleep, so he might as well fire up his laptop and start searching databases.

Maybe he should drop onto the couch and try to catch some shuteye first. He could almost hear a baby crying, which was a sound from his nightmares and a sure sign he was exhausted.

When his hand touched the door handle, Wrangler suddenly stopped and turned toward the yard, a low growl rumbling in his throat.

Eli looked at his partner. Where the K-9 had been relaxed before, he was now all potential energy, his muscles tensed and ready to run. Wrangler pulled his attention from the yard to look up at Eli, clearly waiting for a command.

What did he hear? Or smell?

Eli wrinkled his nose. Wrangler's sense of smell was epic, and there was no telling what he'd detected, even in the still air.

The K-9 didn't typically alert to wildlife...only when he sensed that someone might be in danger.

Holding a flat palm toward his partner, Eli commanded him to be silent and wait. "Wrangler, *stil*." Like some working K-9s, Wrangler had been trained in Dutch to prevent confusion if other people tossed out commands.

From the left, a soft crashing sound came from a distance. An infant wailed.

That wasn't in his head. The cry was real, and Wrangler knew it.

Stepping off the porch, Eli eased into a shadow close to the house, where the light over the barn door didn't reach.

The cries grew louder, a surreal sound in the still night. Crashing feet pounded the ground. Branches cracked. There was a baby in his woods, but was it...running?

Trying to shake the mental image, he commanded Wrangler to stay, then crept toward the sound. Had the kidnapper they were hunting stumbled into his yard? How was that possible?

A figure burst out of the trees and into the illumination

from the barn's security light. It was a woman, and she was clearly at the end of her strength and stumbled, weighed down by a large backpack and an infant cradled to her chest in a carrier.

Was that— "Carly?"

She whirled toward him. Her dark brown hair straggled in tendrils around her face, and her blue eyes were wide with panic. She heaved breaths as though each was her last. "Eli… A man…" He met her halfway into the yard.

"A man what?" He tilted his head and surveyed her. "Carly, what's—" More footfalls in the woods cut him off. Instinctively, he shoved Carly behind him and drew his weapon.

On the porch, Wrangler growled. He was ready for whatever came next.

A man raced into the clearing, skidding to a stop when he spotted Eli. He was bald, but shadows obscured his facial features.

Whatever was happening, it wasn't good. What did this man want? Was the illegal adoption ring now trying to abduct a baby from someone alive and well? And why was his neighbor and occasional running partner carrying an infant?

None of that mattered now. He had to protect Carly and the child. "Oak City Police. Stop where you are and hold your hands up!"

The man remained at the edge of the woods and seemed to consider his options. He took one more step, his arms out to his sides as though he was going to surrender.

When Eli stepped toward him, the man bolted toward the barn.

"Wrangler! *Stellen! Stellen!*"

His partner fired off the porch at the *attack* command, eating up the ground between himself and Carly's pursuer, barking as though he could chew the entire world into bite-size pieces.

It was a terrifying sight that sent the man into a panic. He slid inside the barn and slammed the sliding doors shut just as Wrangler reached them.

The K-9 pawed at the door, his barks fierce, his jumps high. Given enough time, he might claw the building down.

But too much go-time wasn't good for him.

"Wrangler, *kom hier*."

Reluctantly, his partner trotted to Eli's side, nose toward the barn, ears and tail at attention. He looked up, quivering with excitement and ready for a command or a reward.

He'd have to wait a moment for a treat. The danger was too real.

Keeping his eyes on the barn, he spoke over his shoulder to Carly. "Go in the house. Lock the door. I have a landline. Call 911."

She hesitated, still breathing heavily.

"I can't—"

"Go!"

She jumped at the sharp command, but she moved.

He waited for the door to shut behind her, feeling briefly sorry that he'd shouted, but the threat was real. That guy was in his barn, and there were any manner of sharp instruments that he could come out and attack them with if he wasn't carrying a weapon of his own.

He could also escape out the back door, but it squeaked so loudly that everyone in a two-mile radius would know he'd chosen that exit.

No, the man was still inside, likely ready to pounce.

He looked down at Wrangler and back at the porch. Pointing toward the door to the house, he commanded the K-9 to guard. "Wrangler, *yacht*."

Immediately obedient, Wrangler trotted to the bottom of the stairs, his focus on Eli. If anyone else went toward the door, Wrangler would handle him quickly.

Weapon raised, Eli crept toward the barn. "Oak City Police! Come out with your hands where I can see them!"

Silence.

He could burst in, but that severely elevated the risk of someone getting injured.

He could wait. If Carly had done as he'd said, then backup would be here eventually, though it would take time.

He tried once more. "Oak City Police! Come out—"

The barn door slid open, but no one appeared.

Eli gripped his pistol. Maybe the man was afraid that Wrangler was ready for round two.

Or maybe he'd planned something.

Eli was in the middle of the yard with no cover, a sitting duck. "Oak City Pol—"

An engine roared, and the ATV that Eli used to ride the property's fence line roared out, aiming for the side yard instead of him.

He couldn't shoot. This wasn't an attack. It was an escape.

A four-wheeled, horsepower-driven escape that neither he nor Wrangler could stop.

Holstering his pistol, Eli muttered with unintelligible anger and turned toward the house as the engine vanished into the distance.

He'd had a suspect in his hands, a man who'd been bent on attacking a woman and a child…

And once again, he'd failed.

TWO

Huddled in the bathtub with Ariel snuggled close, Carly whispered prayers over the baby who was now hers to comfort and care for, trying in vain to relax so Ariel wouldn't pick up on her fear.

Gradually, although she was surely still hungry, Ariel's cries downshifted into snuffling whimpers.

Carly's back and shoulders ached from the fifteen-plus pounds of baby in the front carrier and the unknown weight of Ariel's backpack, but she didn't dare take them off. If she had to run, she wanted Ariel as secure as possible so that man couldn't rip her away.

An engine raced past the window and into the distance, snapping Carly's head up. What had happened? Was Eli okay? Had she put him in danger?

She swallowed. He was in law enforcement. Should she worry?

Lord, keep us safe. Keep Eli safe. Stop that man before he hurts Ariel. She'd been praying on a nonstop loop since her feet had started running. The prayers were as babbling as Ariel's sputtering gibberish, but she had no doubt God understood.

A soft sound from the kitchen made her hold her breath and snuggle Ariel closer. The back door squeaked open. Footsteps paced on the hardwood. Was it Eli, or had that man subdued him and entered the house?

Please, God. Please...

Canine toenails tapped on the floor. *Wrangler.*

They were safe.

She drew in a deep breath, exhaled slowly, then tried to stand.

She couldn't. The weight of baby and backpack coupled with the awkward way she'd tucked her legs beneath her had essentially rendered her incapable of movement.

On top of everything else, this was humiliating.

The footsteps stopped. "Carly?" Eli's voice rose in concerned question. "He's gone. Where are you?"

"In the bathtub." Now that the danger had passed and her adrenaline ebbed, this was awkward. She was huddled in her neighbor's bathroom, unable to stand. *Great.*

He appeared in the doorway with Wrangler at his heels. His reddish-blond hair was tousled as though he'd run his hands through it, and his brown eyes were intense. At the sight of her, he lifted an eyebrow in question. "You good?"

"Yeah."

"Smart move taking refuge in the bathtub. That's one of the safest places in the face of pretty much any kind of danger from tornadoes to, well, humans."

"I watch a lot of crime shows. They're always shoving people into tubs when the shooting starts." She tried to shuck off the backpack so she could stand, but the cramped bathtub made movement impossible. The easiest thing would be to unstrap Ariel and hand her off to Eli. She reached for the clasp at her shoulder. "Can you take her for a second?"

Eli froze as though she'd asked him to hold a grenade with the pin pulled. His face actually went white. That was something she'd never seen before.

His mouth opened, then closed, and he looked away toward the bathroom window. "How about I, uhm…" He held up his hand and waved it between them like he was trying to shove something out of the way. "How about I take the… the backpack? Instead?"

The man was afraid to hold a baby. *Noted.*

He wouldn't be the first. She'd been around when Mike's buddies visited after Ariel was born. The never-been-a-dad guys in the group had treated Ariel like she'd break if they breathed wrong, and some had refused to even stand near her. "Okay."

He moved toward her slowly, his gaze locked on the backpack, and helped her slide it from her shoulders. As soon as it was clear, he turned and left the room.

She'd never pegged him as rude, but she was shocked he'd walked out without helping her up.

It was awkward, but she managed to get to her knees, then to her feet, and to make her way up the hallway.

Eli wasn't in the living room or the kitchen, though the backpack-slash-diaper bag was on the round wooden table. Unsnapping the carrier, she shifted Ariel to her hip, relishing cool air where the warm baby had been.

She ought to be scared, but numbness had kicked in. She was exhausted, weak and empty. She had a baby to feed and change, and then she had to figure out what came next. Was it smart to go home? Should she go to Wendy's? Could she handle the memories there, or would that man show up in the dark of the night to steal Ariel?

Was anywhere safe?

Ariel wailed, so Carly swallowed her fear and started a running dialogue with the baby. "I know you're hungry. We have a nice bottle and maybe some carrots, if you want to try those." She glanced around as she jiggled Ariel on one hip and dug through the bag with her free hand. The walls were a pale yellow that would have been cheery at any other time. A bar separated the dining area from the kitchen, and the decor was…

Well, Eli had either bought the house from someone who'd never bothered to redecorate or he was very into 1970s retro. It was oddly comforting, making her feel like she was in her grandmother's house, the one place where she'd felt safe until a heart attack stole that safety when Carly was nine. The wooden fork and spoon hanging on the wall were nearly identical to a set her great-grandmother had gifted to her grandmother.

Carly shook off the nostalgia then headed for the sink and mixed a bottle. Wendy had started introducing Ariel to pureed foods a few weeks earlier, and carrots seemed to be a favorite, given how many containers had been in Wendy's kitchen.

But how much? She'd never paid attention to how Wendy had fed her daughter and never imagined she'd be the one in charge. It was overwhelming and terrifying even without a strange man trying to—

Carly pulled in a deep breath and released it as Ariel fussed. The last thing this sweet girl needed was more stress in her tiny life.

Shaking the bottle, she checked to make sure it was mixed properly, then popped the lid and presented it to her charge, who did her best to help hold it as Carly sank into a kitchen chair.

"You guys okay?"

Her head jerked up at Eli's voice from the entrance to the hallway. He stood awkwardly with his arms crossed over his chest, shifting from one foot to the other. Far from the confident officer she'd witnessed earlier or the accomplished horseman she'd worked with when one of his animals had almost gone down with an infection, he seemed ill-at-ease, unable to look directly at her.

"We're good."

"Did you call the police?" He looked in her direction then away, seeming to find the refrigerator incredibly interesting. "They should be—"

"No." Her priority had been getting Ariel to safety. As for the Oak City PD... "I wasn't comfortable calling the police."

That got his attention. His head swung toward her, his jaw almost slack. "What? Why? Carly..." He dragged his hand through his hair as he strode toward the phone on the wall by the bar, an anomaly in a digital world. "A man tried to—"

"I can't." How could she make him understand when he was a police officer himself, even if he wasn't currently working with Oak City? "You might be the only one I can trust." Maybe Wendy had been wrong. Maybe her best friend had been grief-stricken and paranoid after Mike's death in the line of duty. But her friend hadn't trusted the police after her husband had died while sitting in a patrol car on his lunch break. Wendy had been wary, suspicious of Mike's fellow officers, though she'd said little about why.

Eli hesitated for a long moment before he cautiously pulled out a chair on the other side of the table and slid into it. When he sat, Wrangler trotted from the hall and lay down on a bed in the corner, relaxed but alert.

Eli looked her in the eye for the first time since he'd walked into the room. "The only one you trust?"

Ariel seemed to be content with her bottle, unfazed by the tension in the room. "Wendy was afraid of someone in the police department."

Eli's head jerked back. His forehead wrinkled. "Who?"

"I don't know." She rocked back and forth slowly, Ariel

relaxing in her arms as her belly filled and her eyes grew heavy. "Internal Affairs showed up at the house the day after Mike was killed. They had a warrant, and they went through everything. They took his personal phone, his work phone, his computer…" She sniffed angry tears. Hadn't Wendy been through enough? What had they been looking for? "It was hard. If they were looking for a reason he died or something… I mean, is that standard? Do they just show up and go through everything when a police officer dies?"

"You're sure it was IA?" He asked the question slowly, as though he was thinking it through.

"Yeah."

"That's not standard procedure." He said it gently, as though he was breaking bad news.

"I figured not." She'd hoped against hope, but… Her heart cracked a little more.

"And Wendy was scared of someone?" He was leading, coaxing.

She was too tired to care if he was digging, and honestly, he was the only officer she'd trust. He was her neighbor. They'd been running together in the mornings since they'd crossed paths on the road when he moved in a year earlier. They often ran into one another around town and, if they were in the coffee shop at the same time, grabbed a table together for a quick chat. Though he'd shared few personal details over the past year, he'd been friendly and warm.

She'd spent three nights sleeping in Eli's barn a few months earlier when Thunder had been sick, treating the horse around the clock. Eli had spent his off time there, too, and they'd talked through the dark hours of the night. He'd seemed incredibly attached to the animal, willing to part with whatever funds it would take to save him.

So, yes. He was the only one she'd trust.

Carly shifted Ariel, and the baby stirred, took a few more sleepy sucks from her bottle, then relaxed. Carly let her keep a grip on the bottle, already knowing that pulling it away too soon would result in a noisy jolt back into consciousness. "Wendy never said it in so many words, but she started talking more about me being Ariel's guardian if anything happened to her, made me promise to 'raise her right.' She kept saying that. 'Raise her right.' And once, she told me straight-out that if anything happened to her, I shouldn't trust anyone that Mike worked with, especially not with Ariel." There had been a tinge of fear in Wendy's demand that day, and Carly had thought it was grief talking.

Until tonight, when those fears began to live and breathe. "That man tonight, he tried to tell me that he was Ariel's guardian, but that can't be right. I've seen the paperwork. I know what's true." So why was someone trying to make her believe a lie?

The things Carly had said earlier didn't make sense.

Then again, right about now, nothing made sense. Not only had a thug chased her into his yard, but he was sitting in his house with a baby...

...and it was slowly killing him.

He couldn't look at the infant in her arms, now sleeping peacefully in the midst of the storm. It was too much. After all this time it shouldn't be so overwhelming, but it was.

Shoving his chair from the table, Eli walked to the window and stared at the barn, where the door still stood open. He should close it, but he didn't trust that Carly's attacker wasn't skulking in the shadows. Out here, away from town, the darkness was deep and the houses were far apart, offering too many places to hide.

He needed an extra set of eyes until he helped her figure

out a next move. He didn't agree with her distrust of Oak City PD, but he tried to understand. He'd been with OCPD a couple of years when he got called over to the K-9 task force a few months ago, but he'd largely kept to himself. He preferred his horses to people, if he was being honest. And, while Oak City was a moderate-size city and not a populous metropolitan area like where he'd worked in Denver, it had a large enough police force that there were plenty of officers he'd never even met.

He hadn't known Ariel's father, Mike Higgins, by more than sight, though he'd attended the funeral and worn the black armband. A cop's death hit hard, whether he was a close friend or not.

As for an IA investigation into Mike and a search of his house the day after his death? That was a big deal. He'd have to sniff around to see if he could find out more. Working with the task force had him out of the loop on the day-to-day in Oak City.

Would Carly trust his fellow K-9 team members? None of them worked with OCPD, though there were some local LEOs from surrounding areas. There were also federal and state agents from around the region. Maybe she'd be okay with one of them standing guard.

He continued to stare out the window, unable to force himself to look at the domestic scene invading his kitchen. "I've got a friend who's a US Marshal. He's not from around here and has no connections to OCPD. Would it be okay if I had him back me up while we figure out what's going on?"

She was quiet for so long that he wondered if she'd fallen asleep. "I can't go home, can I?"

He winced at the pain in her soft words. They hadn't had a chance to talk since Wendy Higgins's death, but he'd thought of her since he'd heard the news. Maybe he should have stopped by, but the task force had kept him busy.

Too busy for a friend?

She'd lost her closest friend, had custody of an infant, and now someone was claiming *they* were the guardian and trying to forcibly take the child? Life wasn't fair at all. No one would ever convince him that it was. *God, You're there, I get it, but really... You do a lot of garbage I'm not happy with.* He believed that God loved him, but he still wrestled with some anger. Deep inside, he knew God heard him, but sometimes he wondered if prayer did any good.

And yet, he'd never shut down the dialogue.

"Eli?" A tinge of hope lifted her voice. "If your friend comes, can I—"

"No." He steeled himself for the sight of the baby and turned to face her, focusing on the corner of the sofa that he could see through the doorway that led to the living room. "I wouldn't put it past that guy to be hanging out in your front yard, and I think it's safe to assume he knows where Wendy lived as well. As tempting as it is to run to a familiar place, I'd advise against it. He knows you're here, but he's less likely to make another run at a cop's house, especially if he sees I've brought in backup."

In his peripheral, her chin dropped. He couldn't tell if she was defeated or if she was looking at the baby, and he sure wasn't going to look straight at either of them. "All I have is Ariel's diaper bag. That might get us through a day, maybe. I don't have anywhere for her to sleep or a car seat unless you go get my car, and—"

"No car. If we move, I can't trust there's not a tracker on the vehicle."

Her head jerked up.

There wasn't time to console her, although rushing ahead

without her on board made him feel like an inconsiderate jerk. Until they could figure out what was happening and why someone would claim to be Ariel's guardian when they clearly weren't, he had to keep moving.

It couldn't be helped. He pulled his phone from his pocket. "I'm calling a friend, and then we'll figure something out for Ariel." Trevor Slate was a fellow K-9 officer on his task force, but telling Carly that might spook her further. He walked up the hallway into his bedroom, where it would be easier to talk without her overhearing.

He was also running away from his thoughts. He had some things for her to use, but could he do it? Could he open that storage room where memories lurked, waiting to leap out as soon as he turned the key?

He inhaled sharply. One bridge at a time. One rickety, broken bridge at a time.

Scrolling to Trevor's contact info, he hesitated. This morning, Trevor had mentioned that his mother, whom he cared for, had been having some rough nights. She dealt with debilitating lung issues from a house fire that had killed Trevor's younger sister when they were children. Trevor had been coasting on fumes today from working long hours then going home to help his mother's caregiver.

Maybe he wasn't the right call to make.

He scrolled to Maren Anderson's number. While she was a police officer, she worked in Colorado Springs and lived about half an hour away. Carly would have to trust her.

She answered on the second ring. "Eli. Did Trooper escape again?" The laughter in her voice eased a bit of his apprehension. A few weeks ago, they'd checked in on a couple of the new K-9 pups in training only to find that one of the German shepherds, Trooper, had pulled an escape act. Wrangler had located the pup fast asleep under a box, but the stunt had been one more point against the pup's K-9 training. It seemed Trooper was a bit of a rebel, and their trainer, Dev Sigh, wasn't convinced the pup was cut out for law enforcement.

Eli's relief was short-lived. "I wish it was that easy. Are you busy right now?"

"What do you need?" Something on the other end of the phone shifted, and Maren's voice became all business. "Is there a break in the case?"

"That would also be great, but no." He gave her a quick rundown of what had happened in the past hour. "I could use an extra set of eyes, if you're game."

"I was heading over to Colt's to watch a movie while we had some downtime, but we'll divert. I'll even bring him along, if you think this woman will be okay with it?" Maren's fiancé, Colt Dawson, was a DEA agent with the Rocky Mountain Division, and had been helping with their case since he and Maren had teamed up to locate her missing sister.

Eli stepped farther into his bedroom and lowered his voice to ensure that Carly couldn't overhear him. "That would be great. If one of you could take the front of the house and the other take the rear, it would make me feel a lot better. But…" He could hear Carly murmuring some sort of song in the kitchen. "Both of you stay outside and out of sight. What Carly doesn't know won't upset her, you know?"

"Understood. I'll shoot you a text when we're in position. And Eli?"

"Yeah?"

"Don't fault her for being afraid. Whatever's happening at Oak City could be nothing, but it also could be something. Take it easy on her and her fears. You have to remember not everyone thinks like us."

He deserved that admonition. Sometimes he forgot that

the law enforcement brain worked differently. "Got it. You guys be careful. And thank you." He disconnected the call and stared at the closed curtains over his window toward the barn in the back.

He hadn't touched the storage room since he'd moved to the farm several years earlier. Could he do it now when someone needed the contents more than he needed to keep them preserved?

He closed his eyes. *What would Hailey do?*

A smile crept up despite his pain. Hailey would have smacked him on the back of his head for not having already gone out there. *Really, Eli? You've got all of this stuff stowed away? You planning to go into business throwing baby showers?* She'd have laughed at him, but then her serious side would have kicked in and she'd have berated him for not passing a "blessing" along to someone else already.

He sobered. A blessing? It felt a lot more like a curse.

THREE

The wooden kitchen chair was killing her back and Ariel was getting heavy, but Carly wasn't sure what to do. This wasn't her house. She couldn't just wander around and look for a place to settle Ariel in for the night, but Eli had disappeared into his room over thirty minutes ago and hadn't come back.

Exactly what was she supposed to do now? Every bit of information she'd consumed over the past few days warned against sleeping in bed with an infant, even one who could roll over.

She had nightmare visions of Ariel rolling right over the edge of the bed and onto the floor.

Until she could move Ariel's crib to her house and set up a proper nursery, the baby had been sleeping in a portable pack-and-play that was, unfortunately, off-limits in her car. Maybe Eli would go to—

The floor in the hallway creaked and he walked through the kitchen, headed for the back door. He stepped out onto the porch. "My friend is here and watching the house. I'll be back inside in a few minutes."

The closed door behind him wouldn't hear her response. *Okay.* Guess she was sleeping in this chair.

Not that she was going to sleep much anyway. It was a

slam dunk guarantee that, if she closed her eyes, she'd see that man reaching for Ariel. His face was murky in her memory, but that made everything worse. It turned him into a featureless monster instead of a man.

She combed through memories of Mike's friends and colleagues, trying to recall if she'd ever seen the man before, but no recognition kicked in. Eli's insistence that IA wouldn't step in under normal circumstances had her even more on edge. What was going on?

Ariel shifted and whimpered softly in her sleep, then settled down, snuggling closer to Carly's chest. She either sensed Carly's stress or she missed her mother.

As much time as she'd spent at Wendy's in the six months since Ariel was born, she'd never heard the baby as fussy as she had been the past few days. It made her heart crack each time.

Ariel missed her parents.

Carly kissed her forehead. *I'm doing my best, little one. I promise.* But she'd never be Wendy or Mike.

Unable to sit still, she stood and walked around the kitchen, trying to ease some of the pain in her back, wishing she could lie on the floor and properly stretch the tension out of her neck and shoulders. It was tough to do while carrying a—

There was a thud on the back porch, then the door opened and Eli entered. He sat a cardboard box by the kitchen table, then, holding the door open with one foot, dragged a larger plastic box into the room before he locked up again.

He stared at the items, not looking at her. "I'll put this in the guest room, and there's a car seat in my car now." Hefting the larger box, he strode up the hallway.

Carly watched him go, then eased around the kitchen table

and looked down into a clear storage container packed with what looked like diapers, baby clothes and soft blankets.

What was happening?

She trailed him up the hallway. Was she dreaming? Because what he was carrying looked like… "Is that a pack-and-play?" The picture on the box looked like the one she owned, except this one was shades of brown instead of gray. "Where did that come from?"

He pulled a knife from his belt, flipped it open and sliced open the tape on the box.

"Did your friend bring it?" That was a quick trip to the store if so. And it didn't explain the clothes or the diapers. "Do they have a kid?"

"No." The word was nearly drowned out by the sound of the pack-and-play scraping against the box as he removed it.

"Is this…yours?" She looked out into the hallway, though that was stupid. Did she expect a toddler to come wobbling by? Eli had never mentioned a wife or a girlfriend, let alone a child.

"Yes."

Her head jerked back. "You have a—"

"No." He looked over his shoulder and raised one eyebrow in irritation. "If you'll give me a minute, I'll have this set up and you can put…" He returned to pulling the plastic bag from the pack-and-play. "You can put her to bed."

Okay, then. Backing out of the room, Carly made her way up the hall, her arms and back screaming. She walked a circle around the kitchen table, trying to make sense of the night, of the conversation, of Eli himself, but she was too tired to think, and the more she tried to puzzle it out, the less sense it made.

On the one hand, he could be kind and personable and

rather funny. She enjoyed their runs together and their occasional conversations at the coffee shop…maybe too much.

On the other, tonight he was a big, cranky mystery. Maybe he was tired, or maybe this was simply how he behaved when he was focused. Maybe having her crash his evening with a big scary man in tow would affect anyone's personality.

He returned and hefted the box by the door. "You can take her back and try to get some rest. Sheets on the bed are clean." He hesitated in the doorway and seemed to address the hall. "I know the past few days have been rough and you're overwhelmed and the last thing you needed was for some guy… Well, you're safe here, and we'll figure this out."

He disappeared into the darkened hallway.

Carly slumped against the counter, Ariel warm in her arms. She looked down at that sweet sleeping face, long eyelashes lying delicately on chubby cheeks. She'd dreamed of being "Aunt Carly" since the day Wendy announced her pregnancy. She'd planned all the fun things she'd do as Ariel's godmother. Those dreams had been warm and loving and safe.

Carly had been abandoned at thirteen and had shuffled around the system, abandoned by her parents, who saw her as an impediment to their next high. She'd crossed paths often with Wendy and Mike, who were also in the system. They'd forged their own kind of family as they grew up and went to school together. Wendy and Mike had married straight out of high school, and Carly had always been the sister figure.

With the exception of a few prideful months, she'd always had a place to belong.

Now they were gone and she had no one… No one except the infant in her arms who was depending on her for love and for survival.

* * *

Get some sleep. We've got this.

Sitting on the edge of his bed in his dark room, Eli stared at the message from Maren.

Maren thought he needed to rest, and she hadn't stopped blowing up his phone about it until he'd commanded Wrangler to guard the guest room door and then shut off his bedroom light.

Joke was on her, though. He hadn't changed out of his clothes, hadn't pulled back the covers, hadn't done anything but sit in the darkness and stare at the wall.

There would be no sleep when he knew danger lurked, and not when the memories and grief he worked to keep at bay were rushing in like high tide during a full moon.

It had been over since a bullet with his name on it had struck his closest friend and led to a car wreck that had killed his wife and his unborn daughter as well as his friend.

That bullet had been meant for him.

If he'd been behind the wheel that day, hadn't let work call him away from—

Rocketing to his feet, Eli walked to the mirror and stared at his reflection, deeply shadowed in the light that filtered through the curtains. It was impossible to see himself clearly, impossible to find his way out of the darkness.

Now his life was flooded with babies. The task force's case involved finding trafficked infants—and a missing pregnant teenager before it was too late for both her and her unborn child. A baby slept under his roof for the first time.

A baby that wasn't Ivy.

His mind drifted back to the adoption ring case. He had one more lead to chase. Derek Rolls's ex-wife, Gwen, still lived in Oak City, but he'd been unable to locate her. Her last known address had been a bust, and even the team's tech analyst, Eva Gomez, was struggling to find her.

They were waiting on cell phone warrants to hit. Maybe they could locate her that way. He'd promised Eva he would make another pass through public databases, such as the state election website, to see if he could find the woman who might be the key to ending this before someone else died. But all of that was taking a backseat now that his night and his emotions were sideways.

He gripped the dresser tighter, his fingers digging into the polished wood. There was a way to help Carly, though he wasn't sure he could stomach it. He hadn't been able to part with the only memories he had left of Ivy, so he'd shoved her baby gear into the barn's storage room when he'd moved to this farm outside of Colorado Springs, seeking a smaller police department and a lower crime rate in Oak City. Opening that padlock and stepping across the threshold had been like walking into an Egyptian tomb. If he hadn't had Hailey's voice in his head telling him it was the right thing to do, he'd have slammed the door and never looked back.

Oak City and his little horse farm were supposed to be his refuge, the oasis where he escaped the pain.

The pain wasn't supposed to charge through his back door.

The pain also wasn't supposed to be the one female he'd been able be himself with since Hailey's death.

Walking across the room to the window, he parted the curtains and stared at the barn, where Sandy and Thunder stood near the fence. In the warmth of summer, he often left them in the paddock with the option to enter the barn so that they could catch a breeze in the heat.

While he'd often met Carly on the road and they'd joined one another on morning runs, Thunder was the real reason he knew Carly well. When the horse had tangled with a bobcat earlier this year, the wounds and resulting infection had nearly taken Thunder out. Knowing she was a large-animal vet, he'd called her immediately.

She'd been his rock for three solid days. He'd insisted on sleeping in the barn with Thunder, who had been Hailey's horse. If he'd lost the big guy, he wasn't sure what he'd have done.

Carly had stayed beside him through those long nights and kept vigil during the days when he went into work. Around eleven on that first night, when Thunder had quieted down, they'd moved past conversations about movies and sports, moving on to life and the future.

He'd let her do most of the talking, sharing little of his life after high school. Hailey and Ivy and his friend Theo were memories he kept close to his heart. Tonight was the closest he'd come to speaking their names out loud outside of a counselor's office since their funerals.

Despite his concern for Thunder, those nights had been the freest, most carefree hours he'd known in years. While his wife and daughter and friend had been near his thoughts, the past hadn't been accompanied by the grief and guilt that usually came calling along with their memories. He'd actually been able to sleep in that barn while Carly kept watch, and that was a rare thing in his life.

He didn't want to consider why.

When Thunder was out of the woods and Carly had returned home, he'd been left shaken by the ordeal, unsure if it was good or bad that he'd felt something close to normal and happy.

Every time he went on a run with her or grabbed coffee with her when they ran into each other at the café, he still wasn't sure.

But he still pursued those moments with her, even though they left him feeling unbalanced.

A shadow moved near the east side of the barn, and he tilted his head to see if it was friend or foe.

Maren appeared at the fringe of the barn light, walking the wood line toward the front of the house. She must have taken the back while Colt took the front. He was grateful for his team. Even though they were on a race-against-time mission to rescue a young mother and her unborn child and to bring human traffickers and murderers to justice, they'd bonded as a family and took care of each other.

Still, he'd never told the K-9 task force the full story about the loss of his wife and daughter and dreams. It was just too much to speak out loud. Even tonight, when he'd handed the car seat to Colt and asked him to put it in his personal SUV in case of emergency, he'd kept his mouth shut, ignoring Colt's silent questions.

There would be talk, but Eli would continue to keep quiet.

He wasn't the man he used to be, and he was pretty sure he never would be again. Maybe someday, he'd be—

In the paddock, Sandy raised her head and shook it before she turned and trotted away from the western fence.

Something had spooked her. Was it animal—or was it human? Had the man who'd been chasing Carly with the baby in her arms returned? And, if he had, was he alone or had he brought reinforcements?

It was likely nothing, but he didn't dare take the risk.

Opening the safe near his bed, he pulled his pistol out and shoved it into the holster he hadn't yet removed. He pulled his phone from his pocket and sent a text to Maren and Colt. **Movement at western fence. Stand by.**

If it was an animal, he was going to feel like the literal boy who cried wolf, but if it wasn't…

His phone vibrated with a message from Colt. Stay inside. We've got this.

Eli shoved his phone into his pocket, itching to walk out the back door and check on his property, on his horses, to confront the threat himself, but Colt was right. His duty was to protect those he'd invited into his home.

Everything had moved so fast. How had he ended up with a woman and child to protect? Didn't God understand he was no good at that?

He watched until his ears pounded and his vision pulsed. He was holding his breath, a rookie mistake. Exhaling slowly, he forced himself to breathe regularly as he waited to hear if it was safe.

Colt appeared in the barn's light, not even attempting to hide his presence. That meant Maren was somewhere nearby, the stealth aspect to Colt's diversion. Either that, or he wanted anyone creeping around to know that backup had arrived.

Taking long, confident strides, Colt walked straight across the backyard, then clicked on his flashlight as he reached the corner of the paddock where the woods began.

Eli watched Colt's light bounce its way through the woods to where Sandy had spooked. The light stopped, hovering in one place. He was probably searching for—

"I've got a runner!" Maren's clear call came from the front of the house on the western side.

Eli ran from the room and commanded Wrangler to remain at Carly's door.

From the head of the hallway, he could see both the front and the back doors. It could be a bluff. If Maren and Colt pursued the obvious suspect, then a hidden one could burst through his door.

Outside, there was only silence. The house was quiet as

well. Clearly, Carly and her charge could sleep through Maren's shouting and his running.

The silence was so profound he could hear his own breathing. There was a small light on over the stove, but he still felt blind, unable to discern what was happening outside the house, if anyone was creeping closer, if his friends had caught the lurker.

He knew nothing. Nothing but that his job was to stand firm.

Stand firm. Don't move. Wait.

He gripped his sidearm tightly, holding it low and aimed at the floor, straining to hear any slight sound. He was tuned in on high alert in a way he hadn't been in quite some time, every muscle tensed and ready for action. Would he whirl left toward the back door? Right toward the front? Would they rush in from both at once?

There was a soft sound from the front door and he gripped the pistol tighter, waiting…watching…

From the western side of the house, Colt yelled and Maren responded.

The back door flew open, and a man rushed into the kitchen as Colt spun toward him, lifting his pistol. "Federal agent! Stop!"

The man, wearing a dark sweatshirt with the hood pulled up and a red ski mask, skidded to a stop, his arms whirling to keep his balance. Wide-eyed, he took in Eli's stance. Then, before Eli could command him to stop again, he turned and bolted out the door.

Eli ran two steps to give pursuit, but Ariel screamed and Carly called his name. His heart raced, ready to give chase.

But he couldn't leave them.

Backing up the hallway, he kept his pistol at the ready and

rapped twice on the door, his gaze never leaving the kitchen. "You okay?" He prayed no one had gotten into the bedroom.

How many men were out there? Had they slipped into the guest room while he guarded the doors?

"Fine. What's happening?" Carly's voice was trembling but strong.

"The two of you get into the closet, stay on the floor and shut the door." He wanted as many walls as possible between them and any bullets that might fly.

A sound from the back door drew him to the end of the hallway, ready to defend.

It was Maren's voice that called out. "Eli, you good in here?"

"Clear." He stepped into the kitchen and found Maren standing by the kitchen table, her weapon drawn. Her honey-colored hair straggled out of its ponytail, and her blue eyes were angry and determined. "There were two of them. They both slipped away. Colt's at the front door." She holstered her pistol and shut the door, then ran her hand along the splintered frame before she faced him. "They're determined, Eli. You can't stay here."

She was right. It was clear these men feared nothing and, if Carly stayed in his home, he was exposing her and the child she cared for to even more danger.

FOUR

Huddled in the small closet, Carly snuggled a sniffling Ariel close, praying for safety, trying to hear what was happening and desperately wishing for a cool draft to stir the air. At least she'd been able to change into the spare "mom clothes" Wendy had kept in the diaper bag. The long-sleeved tee and leggings were more comfortable than her dress, but it was cold comfort now.

Her life was a surreal nightmare.

It felt as though she'd never lived anywhere other than this closet, that her life before had been a dream, and that anything after would be this dark chasm of emptiness. She couldn't even pray anything more than simple sentences anymore. A never-ending loop of *Please, God* ran through her heart, a silent plea to keep Ariel safe.

The overwhelming fear, uncertainty and grief had left her numb. She couldn't think or process. All she could do was wait.

She'd heard the back door splinter. Heard Eli shout. Then silence. And now, the sound of voices.

Footsteps.

Friend? Or foe?

She huddled deeper into the corner, wishing desperately for more protection than the few winter coats hanging above her.

The light came on in the bedroom, filtering under the door.

Ariel stirred and whimpered, struggling to be free from Carly's strong grasp.

Footsteps on the hardwood. Closer… Closer…

The door cracked open and, once again, Eli was looking down at her. "It's safe for now."

It was the strangest sort of déjà vu. Hadn't they just done this? Why was it happening again?

Eli reached out to her, though he didn't offer to take Ariel so that she could stand without the added weight. It seemed odd but, then again, everything about this night was odd.

Holding Ariel close, she allowed Eli to help her to her feet. His hand was warm, almost hot, probably from the elevated state of alertness he was in. "What happened?" She had no idea why she'd asked when she already knew. That man had come back, and he'd been even more brazen.

He released her hand, and her own stayed warm even as the cool air in the room washed over her.

Ariel settled down as Carly got steady on her feet. The baby always seemed happiest when Carly was in motion.

Eli walked to the door and looked out into the hall. "We can't stay here. As long as whoever is after you knows where you are, they're going to keep coming. I'm afraid they'll bring more reinforcements every time."

"It's not me who's in danger. It's Ariel." What was with him? He seemed unable to acknowledge Ariel's existence. Was that why he couldn't look at her? Was the problem Ariel and not her? What issue could he possibly have with a—

With a baby. The car seat… The pack-and-play… The box of baby things…

Carly sank to the edge of the bed, the weight of a thousand questions pulling her down. There had been a baby in Eli's life, but who? When? Where was the child now?

And what was going to happen to Ariel? To her?

She was swamped. There was too much grief, fear and pain for herself and Ariel and Eli. She felt as though she was cemented to the bed, unable to rise.

"I've got a place we can go. If we can get away without being tracked, no one should be able to find you there. It'll buy us time to figure out what's happening."

"But…" She stared at his back, which was stiff and resolute. "This isn't your problem. It's mine. You don't need to stop your entire life for us. We can figure something out."

"You don't trust the police." He still addressed the hall. "I understand and respect that. Who else are you going to turn to if that man returns and brings his friends? You won't call 911." He turned toward her, his gaze on the window. "Unless you tell me you're willing to accept help from law enforcement, I can't let you go out alone with a clear conscience."

He was right. What was her fear doing to her? To Ariel? To Eli? Was it paranoia on Wendy's part, blocking her from seeking help? Or was there a genuine concern? "Do you think I should contact the police?"

Eli's shoulders sank. He stood for a long time before he seemed to make a decision and walked over to sit beside her about a foot away. "I can't answer that question."

"Will you be honest with me at least? Tell me what you think, even if you can't give me an answer."

He stared at the bedroom door, seeming to read something in the air. "Are you sure you want to hear what I think? I tend to be a little pessimistic."

His thoughts couldn't run any darker than hers. "Most of my nightmares have already come true."

He angled his head slightly toward her and started to speak, but then he stopped and was silent for a long moment. "I've seen awful things on the job." He winced as though every bad memory rushed him at once. "Every law enforcement officer in this area is aware of what happened to Mike Higgins. Any time a fellow officer dies, whether we knew them well or not, we grieve. We hurt. We're driven to find out what happened and to get justice. While I'm attached to this task force and not currently at OCPD, I still know what's going on."

"And?"

He braced his hands on his knees. "I think it's weird someone shot Higgins when he was just sitting in his car. There wasn't an altercation or a chase. He was just minding his own business, eating a sandwich. And the other thing… It was broad daylight on a city street and no one saw anything? It seems odd. Not unheard of, but unusual."

She'd wondered the same thing. To her, it felt like a scene in a television show. It made no sense to her, and it had made no sense to Wendy either. She hadn't been able to think of anyone who might want to hurt Mike.

"Now you tell me IA is involved. They had no reason to be at Wendy's if they suspected the shooting was random. I'm sorry to say this, Carly, but…" He glanced at her, then to the door. "The only reason IA would have gone through the house like that is if they thought there was a *reason* Mike was killed. They're searching for something."

The ever-present nausea swirled up, and Carly swallowed hard. As it turned out, her untrained mind had run in the same directions as Eli's trained one. "And then for Wendy to die in a car accident so soon after…"

His mouth tightened as his jaw tensed.

She'd hoped Wendy had merely gotten distracted while driving, but deep inside in places she didn't like to acknowledge, she'd wondered.

Then again, she'd also wondered if she'd watched too many crime shows and read too many suspense novels. People weren't the victims of actual hit men in real life, were they?

It seemed they might be.

"Why do you think they want Ariel?" Her worst nightmares had already come true. She already knew the answer, and she was already living the terror, so she had no idea why she'd asked the question.

Maybe she hoped he'd tell her it wasn't true.

"If we knew why they wanted Ariel, we might have more answers." Pressing his hands against his knees, he stood and walked to the door. "I don't want to rush you, but I'd like to move you to somewhere safe. I'd like to move now while those guys are spooked. I've got friends who have no connection to Oak City PD who will trail us to be sure we aren't followed." He stood taller and addressed the hallway. "You'll have to leave your phone behind, so if there's anyone who might be concerned if you vanish, just let them know you're safe but going out of town for a few days."

Who would be concerned about her? Her closest friends were dead. She'd let work know, of course, and Julia so she didn't worry about Ariel, and the pastor was supposed to bring food the next day. She grabbed her phone from the pocket of her borrowed leggings.

Eli continued to stare into the hallway. "Do you trust me?"

Carly lowered the phone. Even though he was connected to the very police department she was concerned about, she knew him. He'd never hurt her or Ariel. "I do."

Because if she didn't, what other choice did she have?

* * *

The stars were probably offering a bit of light above, but they were blocked by the mountains that rose above them and the thick trees that grew along the valley they wound through. Eli pushed his SUV to its limits on the rugged back trail that had never earned the title of "road" in any way, shape or form. His grandfather's hunting cabin in a valley in the mountains west of Colorado Springs was remote at best, the very definition of *off the grid*.

He was taking a terrified if determined new caregiver and an infant there.

What was he thinking? Time had dulled his memory to the ruggedness of the trek. It hadn't seemed this long or this difficult in his mind.

He'd done a lot of thinking in the half hour since he'd left Maren and Colt behind at the last good dirt road and turned up the trail to crawl over rocks and ruts. If anyone followed them out here, they'd have a rough trip. It wasn't for the faint of heart, especially not in the dark. Even he was gripping the steering wheel extra tight and praying not to slide down an unseen chasm.

Back in the cargo area, Wrangler had given up trying to stand and had lain down to mitigate the motion of the vehicle. Eli had had to forgo his specialized K-9 SUV to make the trek out. It had no back seat in which to strap a car seat. It wasn't the first time Wrangler had been for a ride in this vehicle, but it was the first time he'd been on a road like this.

In the passenger seat, Carly seemed to take it all in stride. While she'd been holding the handle above the door with an iron grip since they hit the trail, she had yet to make a sound. As for his back seat passenger, she'd been asleep for most of the drive. It probably had something to do with the way the vehicle rocked as he rolled over and through obstacles along the trail.

He really should have come out here and done more work over the years, but he hadn't had the strength since he'd moved back to the area. The last time he'd come out here…

He gripped the steering wheel tighter, even though the trail smoothed out a bit.

The last time he'd been here, he'd been with Hailey, and they'd just found out that Ivy was on the way. He hadn't wanted to come out to the remote wilderness, had been terrified something awful would happen to Hailey, but she'd been a rugged explorer kind of girl, and she'd been just fine.

As it had turned out, he should have worried more about her safety in civilization.

The headlights swept across an opening in the trees, and he guided the SUV into a small clearing where his grandfather's cabin sat. The last time he'd visited, he'd repaired the chinking and ensured the roof was tight, but it was never going to be a five-star experience. His grandfather's friend Isaac, a former OCPD officer who lived the hermit's life even deeper in the wilderness, came by periodically to do basic maintenance to make sure the wildlife hadn't taken over. If Isaac had kept up the checks, the place should be clean and safe.

Maybe he should have called ahead, but Isaac didn't believe in communicating with the outside world much and had barely been persuaded to keep a satellite phone on hand for emergencies. The device probably hadn't been powered on since the day it was purchased.

Eli pulled close to the cabin door and shut off the engine. The only light was from the headlights cutting through the trees. Maybe this had been a bad idea. "I'm sorry."

Unwinding her fingers from the handle above the door,

Carly flexed them then looked at him with a question etched in the lines of her forehead. "For what?"

"I shouldn't have brought the two of you here. It's pretty primitive." There was no shower, and water was pumped in by hand from the spring and heated on the woodstove. There was a compost toilet, thankfully, and he sincerely hoped she'd be okay with all of that. A small generator operated a couple of lights and a coffeemaker, but that was about it.

Carly scanned the surroundings. "There's nobody here who's going to hurt Ariel, and that's my number one priority. Babies are portable, I'm learning. She's got a place to sleep, some diapers, and food. It's warm enough outside that none of us will freeze. As long as we're able to get some more supplies for her soon, she won't know the difference between rustic and elegant."

She never said a word about her own comfort. It was a selflessness that awed him, that drew her to him. It was the same selflessness he'd witnessed when she was caring for Thunder. It made her…special.

He didn't want her to be special. Eli cleared his throat. "And what about you?"

"I'm fine." Carly's chin dipped. "Let's just say I've lived in a lot worse."

The already tense air in the vehicle grew heavier. There was a lot packed into that sentence.

He knew she'd been in foster care from a young age. She'd said as much on one of the nights they'd stayed up caring for Thunder. Was there more to the story?

Maybe they were both holding things back.

He frowned. *Holding things back?* That would imply they were more than friends, wouldn't it?

They weren't. They couldn't be. The idea of handing his heart over to anyone but Hailey was…

Well, it was wrong.

Eli glanced at Carly. She was staring out the front windshield, her face a study in shadows. From the moment he'd first seen her jogging near the house, he'd thought she was pretty. Over the months, that opinion had only solidified as he'd gotten to know her heart, though he'd kept his emotional distance.

And yes, he'd found himself talking to her in those dark midnight hours during Thunder's illness more than he'd talked to any other person since Hailey and Theo had been killed.

But that didn't mean anything. His life wasn't meant to have another woman in it, and definitely not one who came with…

…not one who came looking like a life he'd long ago lost.

Shaking his head, he reached into the console and grabbed a flashlight. He opened the door, and the headlights shut off, sinking the clearing into perfect darkness. "Give me a second and I'll make sure everything is good." Looking over his shoulder, he looked over the back seat and made eye contact with his partner, who was watching from the cargo area. "Wrangler, *wacht*." There was no danger of someone coming at them out here, he hoped, but if the unthinkable happened, then Wrangler would follow the command to guard his charges.

As he exited the truck, Eli hoped Isaac had been keeping an eye on things the way he always had. If not, he might enter a critter-filled, spider-infested, dust-covered house of horrors with a generator that hadn't been fired up in years. If the generator was full of stale gas and had been locked up by corrosion, then this was going to be a lot harder than he'd hoped.

He stopped at the door, his light shining on the lock and

his hand extended with the key. Was he like that generator? Full of old junk that kept him from coming to life?

Was that why he was out here attempting to take care of a woman and a child who weren't his? Because he'd needed to feel useful? Needed? Like he was still capable of protecting someone?

He did that in his job every day, right?

His job was never personal though. It was always outside of him, all about other people and not about himself. Even the task force's case, the attempt to rescue a pregnant teenager and who knew how many infants, had only scratched the surface of his emotions.

Was he meant for something more?

He tossed his head as though he could throw away the question. These thoughts were too deep during a night with no rest and an adrenaline rush that had left his mind spinning. If he kept this up, he'd be psychoanalyzing everything from how he drank his coffee to how he folded his towels.

He wasn't that deep.

He didn't want to be that deep.

He just wanted to survive.

FIVE

She'd almost said too much.

Carly watched Eli's flashlight disappear into the small cabin, drifting past the dark windows as he made his way around the space.

At one time, a cabin in the woods without running water or electricity would have been a palace to her. The only people who knew the full extent of her past were gone now. Wendy and Mike had been her family, had known her at her lowest and had cheered for her at her best.

There were parts of herself that she kept locked away. No one else could be trusted. Everyone would look at her differently, would view her as she used to be, not as a successful large-animal veterinarian or even as a terrified new—

Not yet. She wasn't ready for the *M* word. She was the guardian of a sweet baby whom she loved with all her heart and whom life had shattered at the age of six months old.

Never in her life had Carly felt so incapable and lost, not even when she was eighteen and drifting.

From the rear of the cabin, a small engine fired up.

Carly tensed and leaned forward, her fingers wrapping around the door handle. That man had fled from Eli's on a quad runner. Had he made his way here? Did he know—

Overhead lights appeared in the cabin, and Carly sank against the seat.

The generator.

Eli appeared in the doorway and walked back to the vehicle, his stride purposeful. Opening the back lift gate, he allowed Wrangler to get out before he called to her. "You can go inside. It's a little chilly, so I'll get a fire in the woodstove after I get Wrangler settled. Don't worry about your gear. I'll bring it in."

He was all business. Something was driving him, but she couldn't figure out what.

She was too tired to think about it. The short and harshly interrupted nap she'd taken at Eli's hadn't been enough to overcome the exhaustion and emotions that had piled up over the past few days. What she needed was space and time alone to process the fact that her best friend was gone forever. That hadn't even sunk in yet.

But she, like Eli, had to keep moving forward.

This new car seat had a detachable base, so she removed it and carried Ariel inside without waking her. It was a beautiful thing.

The cabin wasn't as bad as Eli had made it sound. It was certainly primitive, and she wouldn't want to live here for the rest of her life, but it was clean. The wide unfinished floorboards were smooth and free of dust or dirt. The walls were rough-hewn logs, but the chinking between them appeared to be solid. The ceiling was nonexistent, just the underside of plywood that met at a point to create the roof.

Two folding canvas chairs sat in one corner near a small square woodstove. A handful of logs were stacked beside it, maybe enough for one night. Two canvas bags leaned against the wall and likely held cots, while a plastic tote labeled *Sleeping Bags* rested beside them.

In the opposite corner, several boards had been fixed to rough logs to form a makeshift counter, and a couple more plastic totes sat beneath it. A large basin sat on top, and an old-fashioned hand pump stood over it. A hand-built wooden table sat nearby. From the ceiling, a single bulb hung with a pull chain attached.

It was rustic and sparse, but it was surprisingly well-kept. Eli likely spent a lot of time here.

At the sound of his footsteps behind her, she stepped out of the doorway, gently swinging the carrier to keep a dozing Ariel calm and asleep. If she could prevent the baby from waking up, then she might successfully get a few hours of sleep herself before the baby's hunger wailed.

Eli walked in, followed by Wrangler, who immediately went to work sniffing every inch of the room.

Without a word, Eli dropped the diaper bag into one of the chairs, then he set up the pack-and-play. He unfolded one cot next to it and placed a sleeping bag over the top. He grabbed the second cot and another sleeping bag and moved it to the small kitchen area.

Guess he was done talking.

Ariel fussed and kicked her feet. So much for keeping her asleep. Shushing to her, Carly carried her charge to the prepared cot, made quick work of changing a wet diaper, then sat and rocked back and forth, staring down into Ariel's deep blue eyes.

Carly exhaled, and a slight whimper escaped. At times like these, when she was eye to eye with Wendy's daughter, the love was almost overwhelming. She'd been wrapped around Ariel's tiny little finger since that first hospital visit six months earlier. Now that the little girl was hers to care for, that *love at first sight* paled in comparison. How could something so tiny command so much emotion?

Ariel's eyes blinked with the heaviness of sleep, staying closed longer and longer before she finally drifted off, a soft sigh escaping as she relaxed and let the full weight of her sixteen pounds rest in Carly's arms.

As she'd done so often over the past few days, Carly prayed silently for Ariel. In some ways, she was angry at God for leaving this child an orphan, setting her up for life without her birth parents in much the same way Mike and Wendy and she herself had struggled. Her heart ached for the pain this little one had already endured.

But Ariel had an advantage. The one thing the three of them hadn't had from the beginning was someone who loved them and cared for them. Carly was determined to be that for Ariel. She'd never leave her behind. Together, they'd build a family, they'd—

A shift in the air silenced her prayers. The room had gone still.

She pulled her gaze up to find Eli standing on the other side of the room, the sleeping bag he gripped unrolled and dragging on the floor. He was staring at her as though he'd seen something that fascinated him yet caused him pain at the same time. His expression was something she'd never witnessed before.

They locked eyes, and he simply stared, his brow furrowing as if he wasn't certain who she was or how she'd gotten there.

She started to speak but, before she could, his eyes widened. He turned his back and went to work arranging the sleeping bag on the cot, shutting her out and leaving her alone.

The darkness was gradually softening, and Eli begged dawn to break and free him from this torturous night.

He lay on his back staring at the roof, the sleeping bag spread out on the cot beneath him. He wished he could say he'd dozed at some point, and maybe he had, but it didn't feel like it.

For the few hours the cabin had been dark, he'd lain awake, his ears attuned to every sound.

All he'd heard was the soft sound of Carly's even breathing and the snuffles of the baby asleep in the pack-and-play beside her.

He hadn't realized babies slept so loudly. Every breath the child took scraped across his heart, resurrecting memories and dreams and pain.

Ivy had never drawn a breath. He'd lost her in the same instant as his wife, just hours before he'd have gotten to hold his squirming infant daughter in his arms.

He rolled onto his side to face the wall. Embarrassment burned the back of his neck even now, hours after he'd been caught staring at Carly. He'd been fascinated by the expression on her face, by her posture as she'd rocked the baby in her arms. It was something he'd never seen and had never even imagined.

He'd purposely avoided young children and babies, trying not to think of what might have been, trying to keep his grief locked away. This was why. Because the moment he saw a mother and child, he froze. His heart cracked for what he'd never been able to hold himself.

He'd honestly never expected to be able to look at a mother and child without seeing Hailey and Ivy. When Carly had looked up and caught him staring, he'd *definitely* seen her, from her long brown hair to those mesmerizing blue eyes that had been the first thing he'd noticed about her. The sight had jolted him to the core.

How dare he feel even the slightest connection with a

woman who wasn't his wife? How dare he think he could protect anyone from forces working against them?

Because of his failure, three people he'd cared about were gone. He didn't need to be responsible for someone else, especially someone who didn't even belong in his life.

Why couldn't God have had Carly run in the opposite direction, toward the Peterson farm? Then he wouldn't have to keep facing his nightmare over and over again.

That was foolish thinking. The Petersons were in their seventies. While the older farmer was a crack shot with his rifle, there was no way he and his sweet wife could have protected Carly and the baby from a man determined to cause harm.

Flopping onto his back, he dragged his hands down his face and wished for even ten minutes of precious sleep.

A tiny tapping sound moved from the corner of the room, and a cool nose pressed into his neck.

Instinctively, he scratched Wrangler's neck as his partner pressed closer, trying to shove his head under Eli's shoulder.

The K-9's occasional antics never failed to bring a smile. It was as though Wrangler could feel when Eli was spiraling and decided to intervene. While he was trained in suspect apprehension and protection, Wrangler likely would have been an excellent therapy dog. He just seemed to *know*.

After a few moments of morning pets with the K-9, Eli had to admit he wasn't going to be getting any sleep. Maybe he'd catch a nap later. For now, he needed to take care of his partner, then split some wood so they could take the edge off the morning mountain chill and heat some water. No doubt Carly would want warm water for herself and the baby and maybe for formula.

A few things from the parenting classes Hailey had made

him attend were starting to creep in. Maybe he could make it through this, or at least help Carly make it through.

He'd slept in his clothes, so he slid to the edge of the cot, tied his boots and crept out the door with Wrangler. While the K-9 bounded in the woods like a puppy, Eli stepped away from the cabin to make a couple of phone calls on his sat phone.

He dialed the team's tech analyst, Eva Gomez, first. Hopefully, she was up early.

She answered on the second ring. "Eli, I don't have anything for you yet." She sounded as tired as he was. No doubt she'd stayed up most of the night trying to locate disgraced OB-GYN Derek Rolls's ex-wife. They all felt the ticking of the clock as they searched for Mia's kidnappers, hoping to find her before her baby was born and she was—

He swallowed the thought. It wasn't one he wanted to consider. They would find her in time and they would rescue her. There was no other option.

Clearing his throat, he moved on to his request. "I know this is kind of beneath your level of expertise, but I need a favor."

"Something easy?" She almost sounded relieved. "Please. If you give me something quick, I'll be your best friend forever. I'm like the K-9s when they don't find what they're searching for and you guys hide a treat for them to sniff out. I need a little win."

"It's easy enough, I think." He hoped. "I've gotten into a situation here, and I need some intel on a police officer at Oak City PD. Michael Higgins."

"That name's familiar."

"He's the officer who was killed a few weeks ago in the walk-up shooting."

"Yeah." Eva dragged out the word. "He was having lunch in his patrol car."

They were both silent, the weight of their jobs hanging over them and the loss of a fellow law enforcement officer sobering.

Eva was the first to speak again. "What do you need to know?" A tapping sound said she was already working.

"IA visited his house the day after the shooting. Took a bunch of electronics and went through his stuff."

"I'm sorry. What?" The tapping stopped. "IA walked in on his widow the day after he was killed and processed their home?"

"It would appear so."

"Hmm." Eva continued typing, but the clicks slowed and stopped. "It just hit me that this is your PD and your people, yet you have me searching. Who are you with and what are you doing?"

It was no secret, yet he wasn't sure how to answer. Eva's question made him feel like he was somehow in the wrong. Was failing to trust his colleagues at OCPD a betrayal?

"Eli?"

"It's complicated yet not complicated."

"Explain."

He owed her that if he was going to be asking for favors. "I have Higgins's daughter and her guardian with me in a safe house." He outlined the events of the night before, including Maren's involvement and Colt's as well. "Given everything that her friends said before they died, Carly is afraid to contact Oak City."

"I can't say I don't understand." Eva's voice was a mumble, and she went back to typing. "It's a little sus that Higgins was murdered by an unknown assailant and that his wife died two weeks later in a single-car wreck with no witnesses. I'm pulling the accident report up first. That will be easier than discovering why IA was investigating Higgins."

While he waited for Eva to do her thing, Eli stacked a couple pieces of firewood to be split on a stump at the rear of the cabin. As soon as he finished this conversation, he'd get to work heating water.

"Okay, Wendy Higgins was found dead inside of her vehicle after she missed a curve and ran off the road and repeatedly flipped into a ravine. No tire marks. No witnesses."

"That wouldn't be a difficult hit to pull off."

"No, it wouldn't." Eva sounded thoughtful. "What would make her miss the turn? Another car? Was she incapacitated somehow?"

Glancing at the cabin to make sure Carly hadn't stepped outside, he walked a few feet deeper into the woods to watch Wrangler race through the trees. "Can you get access to the autopsy report, if there was one?"

"It might take me a bit longer since she only died a few days ago. The records might not be accessible yet. What I just gave you came from a news story. Also, I'll dig into Mike Higgins and get back to you in the next few hours. It'll be a break from searching into dead mothers and missing infants."

Eli closed his eyes and took a second to recenter himself. Eva might know generalizations about his history, but she had no idea how deeply those words impacted him. "Anything on Gwen Rolls yet?" He'd love to find a way to talk to the obstetrician's ex-wife today. If they could get a lead on Rolls, they might find Mia before it was too late.

"Not yet. She's as elusive as he is, but I'm still digging." There was a click and more typing. "Hey, Eli? I just found something."

"Yeah?" Something in her voice stopped him. He turned to face the cabin.

"There was a break-in at the Higgins house around three this morning."

That was a couple of hours after they'd left for the cabin. His grip on the phone tightened. Did someone thought they'd gone there? "Oak City responded?"

"They did. Someone called it in, and they entered the property when they found the back door open, citing probable cause. They report the place was ransacked."

Anger coursed through Eli, hot and defensive. "Who called it in? Or was it an alarm?"

"Looks like a neighbor saw an unfamiliar vehicle in the driveway and flashlights in the house." Eva was quiet for a moment. "I know that area. It's a lot like the road you live on. The houses are far apart and set back in the trees. There's no chance a neighbor looked out their window and saw anything."

There wasn't, although someone could have driven by. Either way, an unknown person had trashed the Higgins house. Was it the man who'd chased Carly through the woods then tried to rush his place? Or was it a ruse so that whoever was behind the strange goings-on at Oak City PD could enter the house and search for something…or someone?

SIX

*T*hwack!

Carly sat straight up, trying to get her bearings. What was that? Where was she? And why did every muscle, nerve and bone ache?

Dragging her hands down her face, she scanned the small room, taking in the rough log walls and the light filtering in through unfinished fabric curtains.

Eli's grandfather's cabin.

The previous night and the horrors preceding it rushed back, filling in the blanks that deep sleep had carved. Had she really slept that soundly on an old cot under a tired sleeping bag in a hunting cabin?

It appeared she had. *Thank You, Lord.* She'd said a lot of prayers in her life, but this might be the sincerest thanks she'd ever offered.

Beside her, Ariel slept peacefully in the pack-and-play. It often took her time to wind down during the night, but she tended to sleep in most mornings, at least until seven or so, and for that, Carly was also grateful.

But where was Eli?

Thwack!

The noise came from behind the cabin. She turned and

set her feet on the floor, prepared to reach for Ariel and run if Eli called out.

The sound came again, but no one shouted a warning. Maybe it was Eli?

Standing, she shivered in the chilly cabin, then checked to make sure Ariel was still snug in her blanket sleeper. Wrapping the sleeping bag around herself, she dragged it to the back door and eased it open.

About twenty feet away, Eli settled a log onto a larger log, then stepped back and swung an axe over his head, splintering the wood. After tossing the smaller pieces aside, he took a minute to watch Wrangler, who was running in the woods, then settled another piece onto the stump.

He was about to draw back when he spotted her in the doorway. Lowering the axe to his side, he nodded. "I'll have a fire and some warm water in a few minutes."

"Ariel's asleep, so there's not a rush." She leaned against the door frame, almost too achy to stand. While she'd love a hot shower to work out the knots in her muscles, she wasn't about to voice that when there was nothing that could be done about it. Right now, she would settle for the pioneer way of filling a galvanized tub with hot water from the woodstove… if this place had any privacy.

Eli split two more logs without saying more.

Should she go inside? There wasn't much to do, and she didn't want to wake Ariel just to distract her thoughts. She stayed in place, watching Eli. "What about your horses?" She'd gotten to know Thunder and Sandy well during those nights she'd nursed Thunder. With Eli's permission, she'd stopped by a few times on the way home to visit with them and offer a few pets.

Would the man who'd tried to take Ariel harm the horses if

he figured out they were unattended? Who was going to feed them, water them, shelter them if a summer storm blew up?

Settling the axe against the stump, Eli swiped his gloved hand across his forehead. "I texted a friend a few minutes ago. He's going to pick them up and take them to his place."

"That's good." At least there was one less thing to lie awake at night worrying about.

Eli gathered the logs he'd split, tossing them toward the cabin a few feet from where Carly stood.

If she had her shoes on, she'd offer to help, but she had a feeling he'd not let her anyway. Instead, she watched him. While he hadn't been a fan of looking her in the eye the night before, he seemed even more reluctant now. He was hiding something. "What happened?"

He didn't answer but kept tossing the logs he'd split. Apparently, he'd been outside longer than she'd realized, because there was enough firewood to last for days.

There was definitely something weighing on him.

Carly let him work through his thoughts. She'd learned with the owners of her big animal patients that silence encouraged them to unburden themselves when the news wasn't what they wanted to hear. Tugging the sleeping bag tighter around herself, she watched Wrangler take interest in something at the base of a tree.

Finally, Eli approached and began stacking the firewood against the side of the cabin next to the door. "I talked to a colleague on my task force."

"About?"

"Mike."

"Oh." The name took some of the strength from her knees. She'd been expecting him to say something else, but she wasn't sure what. "Is this about Internal Affairs?"

"It is." He squatted to meticulously arrange the wood into

a stack, probably so he wouldn't have to look at her. He was big on avoiding her eyes. "Eva and I spoke early this morning. I only have the preliminaries, and I didn't ask Eva how she got them, so it might not be something I'm supposed to know."

Her spine was about to crawl out of her skin. He was dragging this out for too long. "Eli, just tell me. He's dead. Wendy's dead. It can't possibly hurt me to know."

Without warning, Eli stood and faced her, pinning her gaze in a way he hadn't before. "When Mike Higgins died, IA was just opening an investigation for taking bribes from several drug dealers and gang members around town. They wanted to make sure he looked the other way or covered up their activities."

Carly pulled the sleeping bag around her like a shield. "That can't be true." Mike was the kind of guy everyone liked. He'd been the first to crack a joke, the first to diffuse the tension, the first to make the peace. When she'd met him in middle school, he'd already been friends with Wendy. When Carly's life fell to pieces at eighteen and she'd lived the hardest, most terrifying months imaginable, he'd been the one to suggest to Wendy that they take her into their cramped one-bedroom apartment until she got on her feet.

"I don't know if he was guilty or not. An investigation doesn't mean he was, it just means there was suspicion and possibly evidence. But IA wouldn't move unless they thought they had something to go on."

Chewing her lower lip, Carly watched the sun sparkle through a gap in the trees. She was cold, but the day would warm up quickly as the sun rose.

Although this cold seemed to come from inside. "Not Mike. Mike was..." A good husband. A good dad...

A good dad who'd insisted that Wendy stay home with

Ariel even though they'd been a two-income family. A good husband who'd insisted he could make up the difference in their finances by picking up more off-duty work and…

…and it couldn't be true.

"What?" Eli stepped closer. "Your whole face just changed. You remembered something."

She didn't want to tell him. Loyalty to her chosen family, the one that Wendy and Mike and she had built when they were in foster care and after they aged out of the system, ran deep.

She couldn't betray what she was just now beginning to wonder.

Eli held a hand out as though he was going to take one of hers, but then he let it fall to his side. "Carly, if you know something, then you can't keep it to yourself. It could protect you and…" His gaze flicked to the door before coming back to her. "It might help us figure out who that man was and keep you both safe."

Maybe.

Mike and Wendy were gone, and Ariel was her responsibility to protect. She had to take care of that little girl, no matter what the cost. "Mike freaked out a little when Wendy found out she was pregnant. Don't get me wrong, they wanted a family, but they wanted a family when they were more financially stable." The police department didn't pay much, and Wendy's salary as an admin assistant had allowed them to live comfortably for two, but not for three…and certainly not if Wendy opted to stay home.

"And?" Eli coaxed her gently.

"Mike told Ariel he was going to pick up off-duty jobs at ballgames and such so they could prep for Ariel's arrival and so that Wendy could stay home after she was born. He started bringing home more money, but…"

"It was all in cash?"

Carly nodded slowly. She honestly hadn't thought much about it. She'd assumed he was taking out cash when he got paid or was working under the table, which wasn't exactly legal but wasn't the worst thing in the world.

That wasn't what bothered her now, though. "He never seemed to work extra hours, at least not enough to justify what he was bringing in."

"And what did Wendy say?"

Tears pricked her eyes, bitter with grief and, now, suspicion. "She didn't say anything. She never questioned it. She just bought what they needed and, when Ariel was born, she quit her job and became a stay-at-home mom." Come to think of it, though, they'd seemed to have more money than they ever had in the past. She'd been so absorbed with the vet practice that she hadn't thought to question it before. But now? With the world imploding?

Where had the money come from? Had Mike been doing something illegal? Taking bribes or worse?

Had Wendy known and chosen to keep quiet so they could offer their daughter the lives they'd never had themselves?

"Eli, what if my friends, my family, were—"

A buzzing sound cut off the one question that spiked her heart, the one she really hadn't wanted to ask, not if Eli was investigating Mike. Not if he was going to say things that made her doubt the only two people who had always been there for her.

She turned away and walked into the house.

Eli didn't follow.

She heard him answer the phone, but she didn't care enough to eavesdrop to see if it was about Mike or Wendy.

She didn't want to know.

If something they'd done had put her head literally on the chopping block, she didn't want to think about it.

"Go ahead, Eva." Eli watched Carly disappear into the cabin, wishing this call had come later. The news about Mike's investigation had rocked Carly, and he hated to drop the bomb then walk away as though he was callous to the fallout.

Normally he would have let the call go, but he couldn't ignore any communication from the task force when they were racing against time to rescue Mia Andrews and her unborn child.

"I might have a lead on Gwen Rolls." Eva sounded more tired than she had less than an hour earlier, but she was also triumphant.

As she should be. If they could find Gwen Rolls, they might be able to find Derek Rolls, the obstetrician they suspected might be involved in the murders of those young mothers and the kidnappings of their infant children. "Tell me it's solid."

"It's pretty solid, all things considered. Given that I matched social security numbers, we're either dealing with a case of stolen identity or I've finally found her."

"Where?" If she'd found someone with the same social as Gwen, then they were finally moving.

"I cross-checked names of family members, and I got a hit on a Gwendolyn Marker. Marker is the married last name of Gwen's maternal aunt. Gwen works at a diner in Oak City."

His phone buzzed with an incoming text. "I've sent you the address. Emmett wants you to head over there ASAP." Her voice dropped. "You and I both know every second counts, especially as we get closer to Mia's due date."

He did know. Every beat of his heart reminded him. It was like an internal clock ticking down to an explosion.

If they were feeling the pressure, how was Dodger Andrews feeling? The man had poured money and resources into the task force, hoping to find his granddaughter. The stakes were so high, and the days were passing quickly.

He glanced into the cabin, where Carly stood looking into the pack-and-play. He was the only task force member based in Oak City, but he couldn't risk taking her into town. Leaving her alone on the edge of the wilderness felt just as risky. He'd be gone for several hours, and anything could happen, from an injury to a wild animal to another attack.

There was no time to travel by foot and canoe to Isaac's remote cabin to ask him to keep a lookout.

He could pass the buck and ask one of the other team members to interview Gwen, but Emmett had asked him to do it. While his boss had okayed him making Carly a priority, he wasn't on a leave of absence, so he couldn't simply skip out on the task force for what amounted to a personal matter.

Walking away from the cabin, he watched Wrangler flop in a sunbeam at the edge of the trees, likely worn out from racing around in the woods. He could leave his partner behind to guard Carly and the baby, but he'd still need someone here.

"Eli?"

He'd nearly forgotten Eva was waiting. "Let Emmett know I'm heading in to have a chat with Gwen this morning. Hopefully, she'll be working the lunch shift." He certainly didn't want to wait around until dinner or, worse, miss her completely.

"Want backup?"

"No. I don't think Gwen is dangerous. It's her ex-husband we need to worry about. If she's scared of him enough to use a different last name and go into hiding, then she might talk to me if I offer help." He hoped that was the case. It was always possible that Gwen was in on this. Still, the offer of backup gave him an idea. "Who's near me, though, this morning? I'm not comfortable leaving Carly alone. While it would be next to impossible for someone to find us, it's not *totally* impossible."

"Lizzie is wrapping up a lead in Colorado Springs. I can send her to you or I can send her to run the lead with Gwen."

"I don't want to buck Emmett by not going myself. Send Lizzie here, if she's good with it. I'll see if I can drop a pin and give you a location." Carly was in a safe location, she'd have someone here with her, so Eli should do his job, no matter how badly he wanted to protect Carly himself.

Lizzie Reynolds was a Bison Valley police officer whose K-9 partner, a golden retriever named Reena, specialized in tracking. Lizzie was good people, and it might help Carly to have a female around for a bit.

"Sounds good. I'll let Emmett know." Eva was so much more than their tech whiz. In a lot of ways, she held the team together. "Anything else?"

He hesitated. He hated to ask for another personal favor, but he was knee-deep into this thing with Carly, and he needed every piece of information he could get if he was going to make her life safe again. "I hate to ask…"

"More work for your neighbor?" Eva laughed. "Bring it on, Blackwood. Your stuff is way easier than anything else I've worked on lately. I can knock it out in ten seconds. Like I said, I can use a win here and there. Keeps me motivated."

"I owe you a ton of chocolate and coffee when I get back."

"Yeah, you do. Now, what do you need?"

"It's about…" He wasn't even sure he could say it out loud. Having a child in his care was wreaking havoc on his brain.

He cleared his throat. "Mike and Wendy Higgins had an infant daughter. Obviously, when Mike was killed, the child stayed with his wife, but would it be possible to find out if someone else was named guardian by him in the event of both of their deaths? I feel certain Carly has all the paperwork she needs given she currently has custody, but does anyone else have a claim?"

"I doubt it." The words came slowly. "Obviously I'm no attorney, but given that Wendy was the last to pass away, her wishes would supersede her husband's."

He'd assumed the same but, like Eva had said, he was no attorney. "I'd still like to know. The guy who attacked Carly claims to have paperwork. If we can find a will or something else of Mike's, then maybe we can find out who this guy is or why he insists on taking their kid."

"Shouldn't take me long. If they've filed a motion, I can look up the court case. If not, then it'll take me a bit longer. If Mike had a will on file at the courthouse, it's a simple records search. If he didn't file it, that makes it a little harder. I'm guessing, with him being a police officer, he had one. If not, it was highly suggested to him."

Eli had heard it over and over again. *Do everything you can to take care of your family in the event that the worst happens.*

But the worst had happened to his *family*, not to *him*. In a million years, he'd never have prepared for that.

"I have bigger questions." Eva brought him out of another spiral. "Why would someone be this desperate to get their hands on a baby? Was there an inheritance? Life insurance? Some sort of payday that that someone might see coming?"

Eli made sure Carly was busy in the cabin, then walked to the edge of the wood line. "I'm not sure about life insurance outside of the norm. Carly did say Mike was making extra cash somewhere, though."

"And if it was a large amount, that would explain IA looking into him for bribery." Eva sighed. "I hate that, and I hope it's not true. One bad cop makes the rest of us look bad."

It was a battle they fought every day. It was tough to get the public to trust them when bad actors kept poisoning the well.

"Anyway, I'll get on this and get back to you, and I'll pass along word that you're on the way in. Be safe."

"Thanks." Eli killed the call then walked into the house, steeling himself against the sight of a family…the very thing he'd never have.

SEVEN

What she wouldn't give for a high chair.

Ariel wriggled in Carly's arms, excited to be eating pureed carrots. She threw out a tiny hand and smacked Carly's fingers, flinging orange across her shirt.

Inhaling slowly and exhaling even more slowly, Carly closed her eyes and reset her bubbling emotions. Ariel was a baby. She had no idea that her caregiver was at her emotional wits' end or that this was the only shirt she had. While it was a backup that Wendy had crammed into the diaper bag, it was better than her funeral dress. After almost twenty-four hours, she'd burn it in the woodstove if she'd had something else to change into.

"Baby girl, if you keep throwing food, you're not going to have any to eat." She kept her voice calm and bright, struggling to hold the wriggling baby with one hand and to feed her with the other. *Lord, this is so hard.* Bottle feeding was ten times easier, but they were critically low on formula and she had no way to get more.

The diaper situation wasn't much better. They might make it one more day. Ironically, there were plenty of diapers in the container Eli had provided, but they were all newborn and one-to-three-month sizes. In an emergency, she might be able to make do temporarily, but they'd be cleaning up more messes than they had the resources to deal with if they had to resort to tiny diapers.

Eli stepped inside, leaving the door open to allow the morning sun to brighten the cabin. He eyed her struggle, then crossed the room to shove the wood he was carrying into the stove. "You have your hands full."

"In every way possible." Emotionally, mentally, spiritually, physically… The man had no idea.

Ariel squealed in delight, and Eli paused, his head dropping before he resumed building the fire. "I'll have hot water in a few minutes. You can both get cleaned up then."

"Do you happen to have a spare shirt and some jeans lying around anywhere, because that would be even better." She winced. She hadn't meant for the words to pop out, but there they were. In the two months she'd literally lived on the streets when she was eighteen, she'd not had a change of clothes, and she'd have been thrilled to have hot water for a quick rinse. She had to stop being needy, to remember that things could be worse.

It was tough enough as it was.

When the fire sparked to life, Eli closed the door on the stove. He grabbed a large metal basin, filled it at the pump and carried it back to set on top of the stove. "Give that a few minutes." He walked over and sat down at the table across from her, watching the fire. "So clean clothes would top your morning wish list?"

"You'd be my hero forever." Had she really said that? "I mean, what I meant was…" Her face heated, and her mortification notched up to a thousand.

She shifted Ariel to her other knee and spooned a bite of carrots that somehow stayed in the baby's mouth. With a sigh, she forced a smile. "What I meant was, yes. If there's any way to get clean clothes, I'd be grateful. And…" She hesitated. Eli had already done so much, how could she dare to ask for more?

"And?" He clasped his hands on the table and actually looked at her, his eyes sparking with amusement because of her verbal slip. "This knight in shining armor is at your service." The spark died, and he looked away. "I mean, what else do you need?"

Interesting. For a half a second, he'd seemed almost playful before that shadow descended again. Guess they were both feeling over-the-top stress. "I wouldn't ask, but… Personally, I can handle things at the bare minimum. I've done it before. But Ariel—"

"Needs more than we've got on hand." He looked at the baby for what might be the first time. "Yeah, she's bigger than a newborn." He watched her grab for the spoon, then stood. "You're probably hungry, too. I found some granola bars in a storage box and some packaged oatmeal that I can make when the water heats up more. The nearest neighbor must have restocked the last time he was here." He was on the move toward the kitchen. "You want something?"

She wasn't hungry, but Eli seemed driven to serve. It was in his nature. She'd noticed it many times, in particular at his barn when she'd been caring for Thunder. He'd kept a cooler stocked with drinks and had brought dinner and snacks each evening. Denying him the opportunity to help would hurt him. "I'll take a granola bar when I'm finished feeding Ariel."

When he came back, he set a bar in front of her with a bottle of water, then sat down and tore into one of his own. He ate the entire thing in two bites. "I have to go into Oak City and can bring some stuff back when I come if you make me a list."

He was leaving? The thought shot fear through her. "If

you'll take me back into town, I can run to Wendy's and grab everything. There's no need to—"

"No." His denial was swift and brooked no argument. "Make a list, and I'll stop at the store."

The way Eli looked away from her was suspect. This was more than him thinking the house might be under surveillance. She knew him well enough to know he'd have offered that explanation if that was all there was.

He was hiding something. "What's going on?" It was the tone she used with large animals who were trying to act up. Gentle but firm. Loving but authoritative. "I'm not a weakling, despite what you seem to think." It was tough to maintain a strong posture while Ariel wriggled and flung carrots. A dot of orange mush landed on her cheek.

She refused to flinch.

Eli's mouth quirked before he pressed his lips together and took a deep breath like he might be stifling a laugh. He pointed at his face. "You've got a little something right—"

"Thanks." She swiped at the spot then wiped her finger on Ariel's already carrot-soaked onesie. It felt good to smile with him, even if the laughter was at her expense.

"You were saying?" Eli scratched his cheek then balled up his wrapper and carried it into the kitchen. He returned with another bar. This one he ate more slowly, watching her.

She straightened her shoulders. "You're hiding something from me, and that's unnecessary. I can handle bad news." Even if it was terrifying.

He finished half of his water bottle. Either he was stalling to make up a story or he didn't want to tell her the truth. Placing the cap on the bottle, he set it on the table. "Someone broke into Wendy's house last night after we left my house."

Reflexively, her grip on Ariel tightened. The baby wriggled and grunted, then reached for the spoon and shoved it into her mouth, gnawing on the soft plastic.

It wouldn't hurt her.

Not like the news that had just slapped Carly. Wendy's small rented home had been a safe space for her when she'd had no other. She'd lived there through college and then as she'd gotten started in the vet practice she'd one day take over. It had been a refuge after her brief time on the streets, the place where she felt safe…

And it had been violated by faceless people searching for…what?

She bounced Ariel in her arms, reminding herself that the baby was safe, but it didn't help. The one place she'd never felt afraid was no longer safe.

Tears stung the backs of her eyes.

But no. Crying was out of the question. Hadn't she just made a big deal about how strong she was? Melting down would undo all of that. There was no way she was going to sit across from Eli and bawl.

Standing, she walked over and dragged the sleeping bag off her cot, then tried to spread it on the floor with one hand while holding Ariel with the other. She needed to put the baby down, take a lap around the room, do something to keep the tears at bay.

The floor creaked, then Eli was beside her. He took the sleeping bag and spread it on the floor, creating a large safe space for Ariel. He even reached into the pack-and-play and quickly deposited a couple of her stuffed animals onto the makeshift play mat.

Carly wanted to thank him, but the words were jammed in her throat behind the tears. Instead, she settled Ariel onto the sleeping bag on her belly. The baby grabbed a stuffed monkey with soft plastic paws, rolled onto her back, and shoved the fingers of the stuffy into her mouth. She looked up at Carly as though she expected applause.

Sinking to the cot, Carly watched Wendy and Mike's daughter, so much like her parents. The parents who had loved her and were now gone. The parents who may have done something illegal. The parents whose house had been sullied by—

The tears came, swift and with no way to stop them. Before she could scare Ariel with the violence of her emotions, Carly walked to the cabin door and buried her face in her hands, watching Ariel over her fingers as tears slipped hot between them.

"Hey." Eli was there before she could even register he'd moved. He pulled her close and wrapped his arms around her, her hands against his chest and her face buried in her palms as she wept. She should be mortified and humiliated.

Instead she felt safe. Protected. Sheltered. She could cry here, could release the pain here, and somehow she knew this man would understand.

It had been too long since someone had held her and put her needs first. Too long since she'd dared to cry in front of someone. All her life, she'd hidden in the corners of bedrooms or bathrooms or in her car to shed her tears.

It was freeing to pour the pain out with someone to support her.

Maybe, despite losing nearly everyone she cared about, she wasn't as alone as she'd thought.

He hadn't held a crying woman in his arms since Hailey had a late-pregnancy meltdown when the local ice cream shop stopped carrying frozen hot chocolate.

He rested his chin on Carly's head, surprised that the memory brought a smile and not pain. They'd laughed at what Hailey had referred to as "high drama" after, and he'd taken her for a chocolate milkshake that she'd declared was not nearly as good but would have to do.

He'd always assumed touching another woman would make him feel the same incredible guilt that he felt when the grief downshifted, but it didn't. Instead, holding Carly as she cried over her friends' deaths and the emotions of the past sixteen or so hours made him feel like he was contributing, helping, doing something more useful than he'd done in years. It sparked a warmth in his chest that he hadn't felt since the phone call about the death of his dreams.

He'd stand here with Carly forever and let her work through her pain if it took that long. She'd stood by him when Thunder was in danger. He could finally return that favor.

When his family had tried to comfort him after Hailey and their baby passed, he'd shoved them all away. Now, with Carly releasing her emotions all over his shirt, he was starting to see that trying to do it all himself had been a roadblock to healing.

Maybe he wanted to heal. Hailey would have his head if she thought he was still banging his forehead against a wall, wouldn't she?

The thought rattled him. As Carly's tears subsided, he stepped back and went to the kitchen. When he returned, he shoved a roll of paper towels into her hands.

She sniffed, and it almost sounded like a laugh. "Seriously? The whole roll? Is it that bad?"

If she was going to make light of it, he would follow her lead. "They're not for you. I need you to hold them for me so I can dry my shirt."

Her cheeks pinked. Tearing off a couple of paper towels for herself, she shoved the rest at him. "I'm so sorry."

"Don't be. You needed that." He had, too. He took the

paper towels and held the roll between them, unsure of what to say. There was a part of him that felt like if she'd felt comfortable enough to cry, then he should share something of his past, too. Or maybe he just felt close to someone for the first time in years.

The need to unburden himself pushed against his rib cage. He took a deep breath and turned so that he stood beside her, watching Ariel roll onto her stomach and try to crawl. "The baby stuff? In that bin?"

Carly stiffened slightly, as though she was prepared to take a blow for him. "You had a daughter?" Her voice was low, reverent, as though she understood this was hallowed ground.

Something in her quiet acceptance, the way she asked the question as though it was a precious thing, loosed his tongue in a way nothing else ever had.

"I lost my wife and daughter several years ago when my wife was nine months pregnant." There was no need for details. He refused to trauma-dump on her. What he'd said was more than enough. He didn't want platitudes or empty words anyway. He wasn't even sure why he'd thought she needed to know. Few people in his circle did.

For several heartbeats, Carly simply watched Ariel chew on her stuffed animal. "This must be hard for you."

Eli's chin dropped to his chest and, for the first time in a long time, he felt the sting of tears at the back of his nose. It wasn't grief, though—it was the relief of being understood. Maybe it was because her own pain was so raw, but Carly had heard the things he wasn't saying and seemed to know instinctively what he needed.

Acceptance. Understanding. To be seen.

He sniffed and managed a small smile. "It's definitely not the easiest thing I've ever done." For the first time, he allowed himself to really look at the baby that had literally crashed into his world. "She's cute." It was the first time he'd been able to look at an infant without feeling a stake of guilt drive through his heart. "She's been through a lot to be so little."

"It breaks my heart." Carly looked sideways at him. "I'm genuinely sorry to have dragged you into my drama."

Wrapping an arm around her shoulders, he pulled her to his side, wanting to assuage her guilt. "It's fine. Really. I'm glad I can help."

For a second, she leaned into him, but then she pulled away to pick up Ariel and move her back to the center of the blanket before she could do her funky little dragging crawl onto the hardwood.

The kid really was kind of cute. She was funny, too. Maybe—

His phone buzzed, reminding him this wasn't a light little moment. He was supposed to be on the road to Oak City in the pursuit of a kidnapper and killer, and the clock was ticking. With a nod to Carly, he answered the phone and walked toward the back door. "Eva. You're blowing up my phone today. You're clearly thriving on the work."

"Yeah, yeah, yeah." He could almost see her waving him off. "I told you these were quick database searches. You have yet to challenge me this morning."

"What have you got?"

"First of all, Lizzie is headed your way. Expect her within the hour."

"Good." He'd pass that along to Carly. "And can you let Lizzie know to take it easy? It's a rough ride out here, and—" A presence at his shoulder made him pause. "Hang on one second." When he turned, Carly was standing right behind him.

She had that look on her face again, the one that said he

needed to take her seriously. "I told you earlier not to think I can't handle anything that comes my way. If that's about Ariel, I want you to put it on speaker."

His eyebrow went up again. She was a constant surprise, if a little demanding, though he couldn't deny she'd earned it.

In his ear, Eva whistled low. "I like her. She's a take-charge kind of girl. She puts you in your place."

"Enough already. Is this about the Higgins family?" If not, then he wouldn't allow Carly to listen in.

"It is. You can put her on speaker, at least for the first part. The second part gets a little dicey."

That was all they needed, more surprises. He pulled the phone from his ear and hit the speaker button. "Okay, you've got me and Carly Mayor, the godmother of the Higgins baby."

Carly winced slightly, but she didn't speak.

Yeah, even he heard it now, the reluctance to speak the baby's name. Possibly, it was his way of distancing himself. He hadn't seen a grief counselor in a couple of years. Maybe he needed to hash this out with someone again, get some outside opinions on his mental blocks.

When had he become so self-aware? It made him feel weird, like the walls he'd erected to protect himself needed some shoring up.

"Carly, hi." Eva was ready to roll. "My name's Eva Gomez. I officially work for the Denver Police Department as a tech analyst, but I'm currently assigned to the task force. Are you okay talking to me?"

If Eva was in the room, Eli would slap her a big old high five. She understood Carly's reluctance to trust the police and wanted to be sure everything was comfortable for her.

Swallowing so hard it was audible, Carly nodded. "I'm good. I'd like to know everything you know about Wendy and Mike and Ariel, please."

"I'm here for you." A few clicks sounded as Eva worked at her computer. "I was able to pull both Mike's and Wendy's wills from the system, though I'm sure you've received a copy of Wendy's already. At any rate, Mike's will left everything to Wendy as his primary and to Ariel if anything happened to both of them simultaneously. Wendy's was the same. Everything to her spouse if she preceded him in death, and everything to Ariel if not. Both named you as the guardian of their daughter should anything happen to the two of them, and neither of them listed a secondary to you. You're it."

Carly nodded slowly. "So no one should be able to show up with any sort of documentation that would allow them to legally take Ariel from me?"

"No. There's nothing else on record. The only trouble you could possibly run into is if Mike or Wendy drafted another will and had it signed and notarized but not filed with the court. That's something that likely would have been in their house somewhere. Given that they worked with an attorney on their wills, updated them after Ariel was born and had them entered into public record, I doubt they made new wills under the table in the past six months."

"So that man was lying." Carly addressed the phone as though Eva could see her. "I figured, but I wasn't sure. What I don't understand is why. Why would he want Ariel? It's not like she had an inheritance. There was some life insurance. Some of it goes toward her care now, but the bulk of it moves into a trust she can't touch for years. Some will pay for college, some will come to her after she graduates. That's a long game to be playing if this is about money."

Silence from the phone spoke more than words ever could. Eva had dug up something more, the "second part" she'd warned Eli might be hard for Carly to hear. Should he take the call into private mode or should he risk letting Carly listen?

Whatever Eva had to say, it was about Carly and Ariel. She had every right to hear, no matter how difficult it was. "You've got more. Go ahead and say it."

"Carly, I'm sorry. This is a tough one." Eva's voice was slow, as though she wanted to ease Carly into the news.

"I'm ready." Carly didn't look ready. The lines around her eyes and mouth deepened, stress and fear etched into her face.

"I did some birthdate and social security number searches, and I might have come across something, though it doesn't explain everything." Eva paused as though she really didn't want to deliver the news. "Someone using Mike's IP address opened an online crypto wallet several months ago on the dark web. It was hard to trace and took some acrobatics to track down. At the same time, Mike opened a safe deposit box at a bank several hours from here. It doesn't appear that Wendy Higgins was on the account, and he took some pains to hide it, it would seem."

"Okay?" Carly's brows knit together in confusion.

It was crystal clear to Eli. "The simple version is that crypto wallets require a complicated password, one that people store offline. Some people put it on a thumb drive or have it etched into something metal that won't burn. At the very least, they write it down and store it somewhere safe."

She frowned. "Like a safe deposit box."

When he nodded, her eyes drifted closed as though this was too much for her, but then she opened them again and looked at the phone. "How bad is it, Eva? How much money did he hide?"

"Carly, I'm sorry."

Carly tensed. "Just tell me."

"There's over a million dollars in that account, and there's no record of any way that Mike Higgins came about that money legally."

EIGHT

Carly waved her hands in front of herself, half hoping she could wipe away the words that had just been spoken.

The cabin was silent. Eli watched, his expression blank, as though he had no idea how to feel or what to say.

Eva said nothing through the phone. It was as though time had frozen.

Maybe she was dreaming. If she pinched herself, she'd wake up in her house, ready to prepare for work and maybe dinner with Wendy and her small family.

Shaking her head, she walked away from Eli and sank to the cot, watching Ariel work hard at effectively crawling.

When Carly sat, Ariel stopped and reached her hand out.

Carly lifted her and cradled her close while Ariel tugged at the ends of her hair and cooed.

"Oh, little one." She rocked side to side as Ariel stared at her face with a puckered expression. "What did your daddy do?"

Across the room, Eli punched his phone screen then pulled the phone to his ear and walked outside. The low murmur of his voice came through the open back door, but his words were indiscernible. He was probably verifying the information.

Lord, please let Eva be wrong. Burying her face in Ariel's neck, she inhaled the scent of carrots and baby lotion. *Please let this be something that can be explained. The wrong Mike Higgins. The wrong everything.*

Even as she prayed, she couldn't deny that Eva might have hit on a terrible truth.

Footsteps came closer. When she looked up, Eli was standing in front of her, looking down. "I'm sorry. I should have had her tell me first so I could have broken that to you more gently."

"Would there have been a *gentle* way? Softer words don't make the news any easier." When Ariel squirmed, Carly set her on the sleeping bag then stood so she wouldn't be looking up at Eli. She needed to feel like she was on equal footing, not some lesser-than who had to be shielded and protected. "Any way you said it, it was going to be hard."

"There's always the possibility that it's not true."

Carly dragged her hands through her hair, gathered it into a ponytail, then let it fall around her shoulders again. She should have brought a hair tie or a bandanna or something. It was a tangled mess.

Not that anyone was going to see her.

"I don't think Eva made a mistake." She wished with all of her heart she could refute it, but Eva's words were like missing puzzle pieces that clicked into a picture she hadn't realized wasn't whole. "At the time, I thought it was about their marriage and wouldn't have ever considered it had to do with money, but…" It felt wrong to speak of her lost friends this way, but she needed to be forthright if she wanted to protect Ariel. "Right before Ariel was born, Mike got funny about his laptop and his personal phone. He had passwords where he hadn't had passwords before. He kept them in his sight all of the time, and he took them both with him when he left the house."

Those had been dark days. Wendy had grown convinced that her husband was having an affair, but Carly had never been able to believe it. He'd been too devoted to her. They'd been through too much together.

"One day, she told me she was going to confront him, and I guess she did. I wasn't there, of course. Whatever he said must have appeased her, because when I asked her about it the next day, she just told me everything was fine. She still seemed stressed, but she never mentioned it again. I decided if she wasn't worried, then I shouldn't be either." That may have been a huge mistake.

"But now you think it makes sense if he was hiding something illegal."

"It would explain her paranoia after he was killed. She talked about how Ariel would need me and how—" *Wait.* She was saying too much. Eli might be attached to a task force right now, but he was still with the Oak City PD. Everything she said would probably be used against Mike and Wendy, and possibly her.

She ground her teeth together and tightened her jaw. Not another word. She didn't even have proof that Eli wasn't in on the whole scheme, that he wasn't one of the ones who was after that cryptocurrency.

Involuntarily, she took a step back. Here she was, in the woods in the middle of nowhere, with a man who might turn on her. Had Eli targeted her all along? All those morning runs? Those run-ins at the coffee shop?

She looked around, trying to find a weapon, a way of protecting Ariel if—

"Carly?" His voice was compassionate and low. "It's going to be okay." He didn't step toward her. In fact, he took one step back, as though he could hear her thoughts. "You're safe here. So is Ariel. I promise."

Rational thought geared her heart rate back to a normal level. This was Eli, her neighbor and friend, a man who loved his horses and had sacrificed so much for her already. If he wanted something from her, he wouldn't have defended her, and he wouldn't be protecting them or telling her everything he knew.

He wasn't the bad guy.

Guilt over her suspicions slicked her emotions. She nodded and started to apologize, but something in the air shifted.

A sound outside the cabin silenced the birds.

It was an engine approaching.

She whipped toward Eli, eyes wide. "Eli…" Had those men found Ariel? Were they coming to finish the job?

"I am so sorry. I didn't get the chance to warn you because everything happened so fast." He gave her a tight smile and rested his hand on her wrist. "It's fine. While I go into town like I told you earlier, one of my teammates will stay with you and Ariel. She's also bringing my patrol vehicle so I can take Wrangler with me. You'll like Lizzie. She's good people."

The whipping emotions and adrenaline were too much. Carly sank to the cot and stared at Ariel as Eli went to the front door and stepped out. She didn't want a stranger. She didn't trust a stranger.

She wanted Eli.

Everything was out of control. Too much was coming at her too fast. If something didn't give soon, she might break… for the first time in her life.

The outside of the Oak City Diner was nothing like Eli had pictured it. When Eva had told him where Gwen was working, he'd assumed it would be a run-down joint barely staying afloat.

Instead, it was a gleaming showpiece in the center of downtown, one he'd passed many times but had never frequented. He didn't spend much time in the "artsy" part of Oak City, which had been revitalized in recent years to draw tourists. He knew the area, but he'd never worked a case here. His work had typically been on the fringes, the areas where bad guys liked to hide and criminals liked to ditch evidence.

Watching through the large sparkling windows from his SUV across the street, he glanced at a photo on his phone then tracked a waitress who chatted with a couple as she filled their drinks. She was in her mid-forties, her blond hair cut into a blunt bob and her smile wide. She wore what appeared to be the diner's uniform of jeans and a teal T-shirt.

He looked at the photo again. She'd cut her hair since renewing her driver's license three years earlier, but that was definitely Gwen Marker.

They'd finally caught a break.

He reached for the door, commanding Wrangler to wait in the vehicle.

His partner immediately curled up in the back of the specially designed K-9 SUV. With a bed, built-in water bowls, climate control, and safety features if anything failed to work as necessary, Wrangler would be cool and safe while Eli conducted his interview.

Shutting the door behind him, he waited for a break in traffic and jogged across the street. The best way to play this was to be low-key and not draw attention to himself or Gwen. She'd be more likely to talk if she didn't feel defensive.

He walked in and seated himself as the sign at the door directed, choosing a table near the window, which appeared to be in Gwen's section. Laying his badge on the table where she'd see it, he picked up a menu and waited for her to approach.

It was the end of the lunch rush, and only a handful of customers lingered over sandwiches, pie and coffee in the '50s-style space.

"Hey, there!" Gwen strode over with a smile and an old-school order pad in hand. "What can I get—" The words stopped but her mouth remained open at the sight of his badge. She stared at it for a moment before she lifted her chin to look straight at Eli. "Can I help you?" Her voice remained pleasant, but a hard glint sparked in her gaze.

Was it because she was afraid of him or her ex? Was she involved in criminal activity of her own? Would she talk or would she walk away?

He needed to play this delicately, because he had no leverage to make her speak if she opted for silence. Glancing around the room, he made certain no one was within earshot. "If you have a few minutes, I'd like to ask you a few questions."

Gwen tapped her pen on her order pad and sized him up. She seemed edgy, maybe nervous. Finally, she sighed. "Is this about Derek again?"

Again? Interesting. She'd been put in the spotlight before. "Yes."

Her mouth twisted to the side. Just when Eli thought he might have to remind her he was waiting, she caught another waitress's eye and pointed to a couple of tables, mouthing the word *break*.

The younger waitress nodded, her red ponytail swinging, and continued to move about the room, chatting with customers and offering refills.

Gwen slid into a chair across from him and set her pen and pad on the table. "What's he done now?" It was the tone of someone who had suffered long.

"I'm not a hundred percent sure, but I'm hoping you'll help

me find out." He didn't want to lead with the worst, that the clock was ticking on a young woman's life. It might shock her into silence or make her start spouting things that may or may not be true. He wanted to keep her calm and only pull out the big guns if he needed to. "I know he had some issues with the law in the past."

"The drugs?" She nodded, sliding the pen back and forth in an arc on the table. "You know, I thought he was a good guy. I was young when I met him, and he was about nine years older than me. He was friendly and fun and..." She smiled, but there was no humor in it. "He treated me like I was his whole world."

"But all of that fell apart when he was busted for insurance fraud and worse?"

"It did." She looked up from the pen to him, her chin still tucked. "He was writing scrips for pain killers for extra cash. Kept a lot of big-money people in Denver and Colorado Springs in pain pills. Even up in some of the resort areas. It's wild he wasn't busted sooner, the way he threw money around."

Sort of like Mike Higgins. The man had money he couldn't explain, all in cash, outside of the huge sum in his crypto account. It made his mind spin how much underhanded people would pay to get what they wanted, be it drugs or power or more money. "Do you know where he is now?"

"No. I really don't want to." Her tone was matter-of-fact. "My roommate was afraid he was the type to come after me, but he never bothered me once he left. I guess he was done and didn't see any value in me." Her eyes were sad, as though she took that to heart.

If only he could tell her she was priceless, that there was so much more to life than men and money, that her worth came from something eternal in Christ and not from what any man said.

He had a feeling she wouldn't hear it, not from someone she didn't know and certainly not from another man.

There was a wistfulness in her voice that said if Derek came knocking, she might just answer the door. His heart ached for her, but he couldn't make this personal, at least not until he had the answers the task force needed to rescue Mia.

He kept the focus on Derek. "Did he have a vacation home? Maybe in another name? An off-the-grid place or somewhere he might have disappeared to?"

Gwen tilted her head, pursing her lips in thought. "For real, what did he do this time? This isn't about the drugs. This is about something else." Her eyebrow arched. "Either he's actually going to jail and you can't find him to put him there, or he's done something worse. Neither would surprise me." She stood and looked down at him. "But I'm not going to be the reason that he rots behind bars either."

The abrupt change in tone made Eli want to stand up, stare her down and demand answers, but that would never work. All her behavior did was reinforce his earlier belief. She wasn't completely over the man, no matter what she said.

It was interesting that she didn't walk away. Instead, she stood by the table staring at him as though she would listen if Eli had more to say.

He took a moment, breaking her gaze to slowly pocket his ID while he prayed for wisdom. He waited for internal confirmation before he spoke, his gaze on the table to keep Gwen from feeling like he was confronting her. "I'm guessing Derek has walked in and out of your life more than once. Just when you think he's gone for good, he's back with flowers and trips and..." He glanced to her hand, which was propped on her waist. A slim diamond bracelet glimmered on her wrist. "And gifts."

Gwen stiffened and moved her hand behind her hip. Still, she didn't leave. Somewhere deep inside, no matter how badly she wanted whatever passed for Derek's twisted version of love, she knew he was trouble.

Glancing around to make sure no one was in earshot, Eli looked up and caught her gaze. "Gwen, have you seen on the news that some young women were found murdered? Several of them over the past few months. All of them kidnapped and then killed shortly after giving birth."

She swallowed hard and looked across his table out the large window at the street. Both of her hands went behind her back, and he was pretty sure she was fidgeting with that bracelet. "I saw. The Andrews girl is missing. Her grandfather's made a lot of noise about it."

"Yes."

She dropped her hands to her sides and looked down at Eli, the lines around her eyes deep. "You think Derek's involved? Because of him being an OB?"

"We're following a lot of leads, and we'd like to talk to Derek just to be sure." He watched Gwen gnaw at her bottom lip for a moment, letting her connect the dots, letting the idea reach her emotions before he tried to force her into speaking.

With a heavy sigh, she slid back into the chair and rested her hands on the table, twisting the bracelet around on her wrist. "I'm not saying he took those women. I don't know. I really haven't seen him in forever."

"I understand." Eli kept his voice even, though his heart beat faster. Answers might be on the tip of Gwen's tongue.

She stared at her wrist. "His maternal grandmother is in a nursing home, different last name than his. She's got dementia bad. She has a house outside of Pueblo. I thought Derek had sold it to take care of her bills at the home, but…" Her shrug was defeated and slow. "It's possible he didn't."

The urge to bolt from the restaurant and pursue the lead was strong, but he held himself in check. "Thank you, Gwen." He started to rest his hand on hers; the last thing he wanted was to give the wrong impression to a woman who clearly had deep wounds. "Can I ask you one more question?" He waited for her to nod. "Did Derek ever bring anyone around that gave you pause?"

Pulling her hands from the table, she dropped them into her lap, but it was obvious that bracelet burned her wrist like hot coals. "Yeah. This one guy, Benny. I don't know his last name. He used to come by the house late at night, and he and Derek would leave together. Derek said they were doing 'odd jobs' for extra cash, and I didn't…" She stared at her hands in her lap. "I should have asked more questions."

This might be a bigger lead than the house. If they could locate an associate, they'd have a larger net to cast. "Can you describe Benny?"

"Tall, skinny dude. Kind of stringy blond hair and these weirdly empty blue eyes. I never liked to be around him. He creeped me out. It was like he was dead inside. He—" Abruptly, she stood and swiped her order pad and pen from the table. "I need to get back to work, but I hope you…" She looked around the room. "Give me your card."

Eli passed it over, knowing she was done talking for now. "You've been a big help, Gwen. Thank you."

She pocketed his card and dug her teeth into her lower lip. "I hope you find that girl." Without looking back, she turned and walked away.

He headed for the door. With the clock running out, every second they waited to act on this new lead was one less second to rescue Mia.

NINE

Carly straightened from settling Ariel down for a nap in the pack-and-play. Resting her hands on her hips, she arched her back, trying to find relief from carrying the baby around for most of the morning.

From the kitchen table, Lizzie watched with a sympathetic smile. "Babies are cute, but they look like a lot of work." She shoved a metal travel mug across the table as Carly approached. "Offer stands if you want it. I'm sure the coffee's still warm. I took a chance and added cream and sugar."

"I forgot you'd offered it." Walking over to the table, Carly picked up the metal cup and cradled it as though she could feel the warmth through it. When Lizzie had arrived, she'd offered Carly the mug and a bagel she'd picked up on the way in. Carly had managed to finish eating her bagel after Eli left, but she'd had to fight off tiny hands the entire time. "Ariel is wonderful, but on days like today…" On days like today, she wished she could nap like a baby, too.

"It can't be easy." Lizzie's green eyes were sympathetic, as though she understood. "You've both been through a lot. Eli filled me in."

Sitting across from Lizzie, Carly settled the mug on the table, but she didn't relax her grip on the one thing that almost felt normal.

She liked Lizzie. The other woman was a little like sunshine, with her blond ponytail and her ready smile. She was almost too easy to talk to. "It would be a lot easier if we were home in familiar surroundings. That poor kiddo has lost her dad, her mom, her home, her second home—"

"And you've lost your best friend's husband, your best friend, your home…" Lizzie tilted her head, almost like she was reading Carly's thoughts. "…and your second home."

Carly's gaze dropped to the blue metallic coffee cup. Someone understood she'd lost her family without her having to say it.

If she hadn't cried out her tears all over Eli's shirt already, she might have more now. "Thank you." It was the best she could do. The wounds were so fresh that she really wasn't ready to work through them, but it helped to feel seen, first by Eli and now by Lizzie.

As if sensing that Carly needed something, Lizzie's partner, a golden retriever named Reena, trotted over and rested her head in Carly's lap, looking up at her with big brown eyes.

Lizzie chuckled. "She likes you."

Scratching the K-9's ears, Carly focused on the gaze of an animal who seemed to see into her heart. "What's her job?"

"Tracking."

"So you're a brave girl who finds lost people." Carly scrubbed behind Reena's ears, and the K-9 almost melted under the attention. The look on Reena's face actually made her smile. "You're a little broken hearts mender, aren't you?"

"I'll add that to her résumé. It'll scare the criminals to death." Lizzie's voice held amusement, as though she knew Carly needed to keep it light.

But what she really needed was to talk about someone else for a while. She sensed Lizzie wouldn't mind. With a final pat on Reena's side, she sat up and waited for the dog to trot away before she faced Lizzie. "So, what made you go into law enforcement?"

There was a brief rigidness that hit Lizzie's posture, as though the question had come like an unexpected gunshot.

Carly could feel her face flush. Maybe that wasn't something most law enforcement officers liked to talk about. Mike had always been open about his reasons for becoming a cop, because he'd wanted to bring justice to anyone who would dare to harm kids like they had been. Maybe he'd been an anomaly.

Come to think of it, Eli hadn't brought his reasons up in all of the hours they'd talked. "I'm sorry. That might be a personal question."

"It's not. Most people are happy to answer. I just…" For several moments, the only sound between them was the chirping of birds outside. "I've always felt protective of where I grew up, and I knew someone who…" She fiddled with her coffee cup, seeming too anxious. "He was always in trouble when we were kids, hurt a few people even. Made me want to protect people and maybe, in some ways, to intervene with kids before they end up in jail for…" She swiped the air in front of her face, seeming to come back from far away. "So yeah, it's kind of a basic answer. Protecting people."

It didn't feel like a *basic answer*. It felt like something deeper, the truth spoken in the spaces between the words.

Carly let it lie. It wasn't her business.

"Eli says you're a veterinarian?" It was clear that Lizzie wanted to move the conversation away from herself.

"I am. Large animals. I knew Eli as a neighbor, and we'd jogged together a few times or grabbed coffee if we were both in town. When Thunder got sick, I had the time to spend at the barn, so I stayed over there a few nights coaxing her through. Eli hung out, too."

"Interesting." Lizzie stood and walked around the room, peeking out of the windows to survey the area outside. "I asked you about being a vet, not about how you met Eli." She glanced over her shoulder and smiled, then looked out the window again.

Face burning, Carly whipped around with her back to the other woman and grabbed her coffee cup with a white-knuckled grip. Lizzie was right. What had made her start babbling about Eli?

"You know, it doesn't surprise me that he bunked in the barn with Thunder when she was sick." Lizzie moved to the back window, her face illuminated by sunlight. "That was his wife's horse."

The wife who'd died.

Eli carried so much pain—how dare she be drawn to him even for an instant when he'd already loved and lost so much.

"He doesn't talk about her often. I don't know her name or what happened, but he let that little detail slip once." Lizzie kept her attention outside. "He's a good guy. A little closed off, not much of a talker, but a good guy. It would be nice to see him open up. I get the feeling he's carrying a lot of guilt over something, and he needs to let that go. When he does…" With a shrug, she walked to the window closest to the table, but she didn't look at Carly. "I've actually seen him look happier this morning around—" Her posture stiffened. She slid to the side of the window but continued to watch, her hand now resting on the pistol at her hip.

As though she knew something had changed, Reena left her spot by Carly and stood at attention by Lizzie.

Carly stood, fighting the urge to throw herself onto the floor. "What?"

"I have movement." Lizzie glanced at her then returned to the window. "Get low and get near Ariel but leave her where she is. She'll be safe there." Lizzie grabbed her phone, fired off a text, then returned to her surveillance. "Don't worry. I've got this."

But did she? Had they been found? Could a bullet penetrate these thick wooden walls?

Carly crouched by Ariel, desperate to throw her body over the baby's to protect her. Whatever came next, she'd keep her goddaughter safe…even if she had to sacrifice herself.

Eli was a frozen statue in the baby aisle.

In some ways it felt like yesterday that he'd been standing on a dozen similar aisles with Hailey as they dreamed and wished and planned.

Those dreams and wishes and plans had netted him nothing but ashes.

Shaking off the memories, he slid his mind into the practical, forcing himself not to tumble into grief and what might have been.

Carly and Ariel needed him to be present today, to protect them in the here and now.

He glanced at the list Carly had texted. Diapers in the appropriate size. A couple of bottles. Several containers of formula. Wipes.

Basic stuff. Necessities.

He looked to the left. What about a bouncer? It was small and would offer another space for Ariel to settle in. He shoved it into the cart and headed for the food aisles as quickly as he could. More than anything, he wanted to get back to the cabin to be sure they were okay…and to continue chatting with Carly.

He wandered the grocery section and picked up a few

more boxed foods and some fresh items, water and anything that looked like comfort food. While he had to come back and forth to work the case, Carly and Ariel could potentially be stuck in the cabin for days or weeks.

He was headed for the bread aisle when his phone buzzed.

A glance at his watch told him it was FBI Agent Emmett Dane, their task force leader.

Moving out of the flow of traffic, he found an isolated spot and took the call without even saying hello. Shoppers flowed down a main aisle while he tucked away in a corner by the frozen seafood. "Hey. I've got intel on where Derek Rolls might be."

Emmett chuckled. "You in a hurry? Can we be a little less harried?" His tone was light, but it was also an order. Emmett wasn't formal about protocol, but he was big on respecting one another.

"Sorry." Eli took a deep breath. Too many things were coming at him at once. He needed to stop and compartmentalize. Right now, finding Mia Andrews was his biggest priority, and then it was getting back to Carly. Mia's due date drew closer with each passing minute, and if they were too late…

If they were too late, Mia would be dead and her baby would be gone. He knew that pain too well.

The last thing he wanted was to miss anything. "I talked to Gwen Marker and got some intel on where Derek might be and about a possible associate. I sent you an email and forwarded it to the rest of the team as well." He ran down the information that Gwen had given to him about the house and the guy named Benny. "It will take some digging, but we might be onto something."

"Hmm." Emmett's voice deepened an octave, and a couple of clicks said he was into his email, following along with what Eli was saying. "Is Lizzie still at the cabin?"

"I'm headed that way as soon as I pick up some supplies." Guilt stabbed him in the gut. He ought to be focused on finding Mia, but he couldn't abandon Carly and Ariel. They needed him.

He wasn't quite sure how to explain, but he was growing to need them as well. He'd found himself opening up to Carly in a way he hadn't talked to anyone in years.

He wasn't sure how he felt about that.

"You with me, Eli?" Emmett was waiting for something. Whatever their team leader had said, it hadn't crossed the filter of Eli's confusion.

"Sorry. Say again?"

"After you get back to the cabin, I'm going to have Lizzie and Trevor make the run to Pueblo to check out the house. I'll get Eva working on the associate if she hasn't already started. With only a first name and a vague physical description, we might not get far, but it's more than we had before. This Benny could be the key to discovering who got Derek Rolls involved in the black-market baby trade and who's running the show. But man, this is a seriously sick way of doing it."

It really was. How did someone come up with the idea to view young women this way, and vulnerable young women at that? And then to steal their babies and treat them all as commodities? The very idea sent a shiver through Eli. Children were precious, and so were mothers. So were families.

So was everyone.

Around him, the early-afternoon shopping crowd was mostly made up of retirees or young mothers and children, with a few dads thrown in. Standing here with his history, talking about this case while Carly and Ariel were also in hiding, made every single person passing by appear to be in danger. There was a part of him that wanted to scream at them to be vigilant and to protect themselves.

Thanks to the way his mind was spinning, every single man wandering the aisles looked like a threat. There were only a few, but each of them pinged the danger signal inside of him. How could he protect everyone from the harm that could befall them? He hadn't even been able to protect his own family.

Babies. Mothers. They were all around him. *God, what are You doing to me?*

"Hey, Eli?" Emmett's voice gentled, shifting from command to friend. "Can I say something personal?"

"When have you ever hesitated?" He watched a middle-aged man wearing jeans and a gray dress shirt scope the cereal aisle, walking slowly along and searching the options. The man made a selection and moved on.

"True." Emmett chuckled. "Knowing you, I'm the only person on the task force who knows about your family, and that's only because I had to vet you before you were brought on. I won't lie, I had some hesitation given what happened. I was afraid you'd take the case too personally and go on a vendetta of sorts."

The words snapped his head back. He'd had no idea Emmett knew the whole story, though he should have. He'd definitely not known that Emmett had ever had doubts about him. "You want me off the task force? You think I'm biased?" *Or distracted?* That was possible, given that he hadn't been able to get Carly out of his mind for most of the day.

But to think that Emmett might—

"No. Those hesitations were before I met you. You're a good investigator and a good man. Don't let your own doubts start distracting you, though." His tone was light, but there was a warning behind it. *Get your head in the game before someone gets hurt or something slips by you.* "You will always carry your wife and your daughter and your friend with you. You will always love them. It's not a betrayal to care about other people, too. Let your friends in. Talk to people. Don't keep living a solitary life separated from the ones who care about you or who you care about."

In the main aisle, foot traffic continued to pass, but the noise receded as Emmett's words filled his head. "Why are you saying this now?" He'd been working with the task force nearly four months, and they'd never had a conversation like this one.

"It was on my mind, and I felt like I should say it."

Now. In the midst of searching for Mia. In the midst of protecting Carly and Ariel. In the midst of his discovery that he actually enjoyed talking to her...and had all along.

He wasn't ready to talk to Emmett about any of that. There was too much going on. "I'll take that under advisement." He winced. He really hadn't intended for the words to sound so formal.

"You do that." Emmett seemed to understand what was happening and said no more. "I'm going to get moving on my end. You go take care of your current charges. And watch your back. I wouldn't be surprised if someone knows you've talked to Gwen, and I also wouldn't be surprised if whoever busted into your house isn't on the lookout for you to head back into town either."

Emmett was right. Vigilance was key.

They ended the call and Eli headed to the front of the store. As he was tapping his card to pay, his phone buzzed, and he pulled it from his hip pocket as he navigated the cart one-handed toward the door.

It was Lizzie. I've got movement at the cabin. Looks like a person.

His heart picked up speed. He was nearly an hour away. He practically ran through the parking lot, the cart bouncing ahead of him.

At the SUV, he stopped. *Wrangler.* He hadn't even considered that the K-9 would have to share his customized rear kennel with cargo.

It couldn't be helped.

He tried to call Lizzie before opening the SUV, but the call went to voice mail.

His heart hammered faster. Where was she? What was happening? Carly had no cell phone, so he couldn't—

A blow slammed into the back of his head, knocking him off balance and throwing him against the cart handle. The wind shoved out of his lungs. The cart rolled and smacked into the rear of his vehicle when he tried to grasp it to regain his balance. He scrambled for the SUV's bumper, catching himself before he hit the ground. Shoving up, he smashed into his attacker, stumbling them both backward.

Inside the SUV, Wrangler barked, his growls deep and menacing.

Eli righted himself. If he could just get to his keys...

They were deep in his pocket, and he needed both hands if—

The man shoved him again, and Eli rammed face-first into the back window, stars passing before his eyes. There were other people in the busy parking lot. Was no one going to help? His ears were ringing too loudly to hear if anyone was calling out or coming to his aid. Something warm trickled down his temple, and he didn't want to think about why.

Wrangler barked and snarled, pawing at the glass.

Before he could whip around to throw a punch of his own, the person shoved him against the SUV again, then wrapped something around his neck and pulled tight.

Eli choked, gasping for air. He tried to dig the object away from his neck, but dark spots around his eyes were quickly defeating him. His ears roared.

He had one chance. One shot.

Dropping his hands, he clawed for the door handle, then pushed away from the vehicle with all his might while pulling the handle for the liftgate.

The weight on his neck eased enough for him to get a good breath. Before he could fight back, Wrangler leaped to the ground and pounced on his attacker.

A man screamed, and Eli was suddenly free. He ripped what turned out to be a thin rope from his neck and whirled around as Wrangler snarled and snapped.

A man wearing a dark blue hoodie and a surgical-style mask stared wide-eyed and frozen at the K-9. His frozen posture was the only thing keeping him from feeling the crunch of Wrangler's bite. One move and—

A dark sedan roared up, the door hanging open. The man whirled and dove into it, slamming the door as the car screeched up the aisle and onto the main road.

Wrangler's barking escalated until Eli commanded him to sit. Bending at the waist, Eli fought for breath as well-meaning people finally rushed toward him. He waved them off and commanded Wrangler to get back into the SUV. One of them might have taken video, but he couldn't ask them to send it to OCPD, not when he wasn't certain who to trust.

And he couldn't stay to ask. He had to get to the cabin.

He had to know that Carly and Ariel weren't already gone.

TEN

Carly's heart beat faster as she crouched by Ariel's pack-and-play, watching Lizzie. Reena stood at the ready, eyes on Lizzie, waiting for a command.

It seemed like hours before Lizzie spoke. "Stay there." She strode to the door, never looking back. "I don't see anything now, but I'm going to check outside. Lock the door. Don't open it until I tell you it's safe." She was gone before Carly could argue that it might *not* be safe and Lizzie should wait for backup.

Somehow, she had a feeling that wasn't in the officer's nature.

There was nothing to do but obey. Dread pooled in Carly's gut at the idea of being even a few feet from Ariel, but she raced to the door and locked it, then secured the back door as well.

Heart hammering, soul screaming, she grabbed a stick of firewood, dropped onto the floor beside her still-sleeping goddaughter and held her makeshift weapon in preparation to swing it.

The silence was so loud that it was deafening. She wanted to hum or scream; either one would do.

Memories came flooding in. This was too much like the time she'd hidden in a storm drain one night in Denver, not wanting to think what might be creating the dampness beneath her or what might be crawling across her bare ankle as she prayed for safety. She'd been huddling in a doorway on that hot July night, trying to catch some sleep, when two men cruised past and called out lewd, awful things at her. Even from a distance, the car had reeked of marijuana and alcohol. When they'd slowed and backed up, she'd known she was in trouble.

Their inebriation had been the only thing that had saved her. She'd raced down an alley and across a street before she found a culvert and crawled into a space that was barely wider than her shoulders. The smell had been terrible. The damp had been sickening. She'd never figured out if the skittering on her bare skin had been real or her imagination. Either way, she'd dug her teeth into her wrist to prevent herself from crying out in fear and disgust as the men wandered the area, calling out terrible things they'd do to her if they found her.

That had been the night she'd realized she needed to swallow her pride and stop trying to do everything on her own. Mike and Wendy had offered her a place to stay, and she'd waved them off until that moment. When she'd shown up at trainee cop Mike's station covered in filth and tears, he'd immediately phoned Wendy to pick her up. She'd slept on their couch in a tiny apartment that was barely better than the streets…but at least it had a lock.

Like today.

She hadn't felt that sickening, helpless, hunted feeling again until now, not even at Eli's house. There was nothing she could do but wait and pray.

The time ticked by in what might have been seconds or hours. It was tough to say. *Lord, keep Lizzie safe. Why is*

*this happening? Shouldn't we have all been safe? Shouldn't
a home be enough? Hasn't Ariel been through—*

A light tap came from the back door. "It's Lizzie. Everything's fine."

Tension made it hard to unwind her body from the ball she'd curled into. Carly stood on shaky legs and hobbled across the hardwood, gripping the piece of firewood like a baseball bat. She stopped at the back door to listen. What if it wasn't Lizzie? What if—

"It's me and Reena. I can prove it. You dressed Ariel in a light green onesie before you put her down for a nap."

There was no way anyone outside of the cabin would know that detail. Exhaling a sigh of relief, Carly unlocked the door and eased it open.

Lizzie and Reena breezed in as though they'd taken a walk in the park. "All clear." Closing the door behind her, Lizzie locked it and walked into the room with an air that might have been a little too casual.

As she gathered up her coffee cup and moved it to the makeshift sink, Lizzie addressed the air in front of her without looking at Carly. "I talked to Eli while I was out there. He's headed back. He was worried when he couldn't get us on the phone after I texted him and told him I saw motion outside."

Something was wrong. Lizzie was cagey, like she was holding back information. What had she seen outside? Or worse, what had Eli really said? "Lizzie? What's—"

A squeak and a cry from Ariel cut off the question.

Carly lifted the baby and rocked back and forth, shushing her with wordless sounds. It wasn't the first time something had scared Ariel straight out of sleep and into wailing, terrified cries.

Lizzie turned to watch, her brow creased with concern. "Is she okay?"

"She will be." It took a few minutes for an episode to pass. Carly walked around the room, swaying gently back and forth as Ariel reached decibels that were truly unhealthy for her ears. "Times like these make me wonder how her mind works. Does she miss her mom and dad? Does she remember being born? Or is it just some random pain or sensation that jerks her out of sleep?"

"Or is it being moved from place to place and seeing nothing familiar when she wakes up?"

Carly flinched. She might be a new guardian, but the mother guilt was real. What was all this running and stress doing to Ariel? How could she mitigate the shock of transition for a tiny baby when she was still swimming in grief and fear herself?

"I am so sorry." Lizzie stepped closer, wincing. "That sounded really harsh, and I didn't mean it that way. I was just…" She spun her hand in the air. "Brainstorming with you about what might be happening."

"I didn't take offense." Now that Lizzie was talking, though, she'd take the opportunity to get more information. "What happened while you were outside? Was someone there?"

If there was a hitch in Lizzie's step, she covered it well. "No. I looked for footprints and didn't find any human ones, though there were some decent-sized paw prints out there, fresh ones in the area where I saw movement. They're too big to belong to Reena or Wrangler, so you guys may have a coyote or a mountain lion prowling around. Might want to be careful about that."

A chill shivered through Carly, making Ariel's cries rise in pitch. Didn't they have enough to worry about from human predators? As a vet, she'd seen what wild animals could do to domesticated animals. The thought of Wrangler tangling with an angry mountain creature was enough to fuel a dozen nightmares.

Ariel's shrieks intensified, and Carly winced a silent apology to Lizzie as Reena curled up in the corner with her back to the commotion. "I'm so sorry for the decibel level. Sometimes she wakes up and it's just…on. It passes, but it takes time and soothing." It was never a bottle or a diaper change that worked. It always just seemed to pass…eventually.

Lizzie smiled. "You're both fine. I can imagine it's tough to have feelings that you don't know how to express. They have to come out somehow."

Carly paced the room, tired of thinking even though her brain was running in high gear. It could be hard to express emotions and feelings even *with* words. She was proof of that. So was Eli.

It felt like Carly walked and cooed and prayed for hours while Lizzie moved from window to window, watching outside. She really didn't want to know what all the vigilance was about.

She just wanted to go home. She'd barely had time to adjust to the deaths of her friends or the reality of having a baby to care for, and now she was in this surreal place where—

"Eli's here." The sound of an approaching engine punctuated Lizzie's words.

Half the tension in Carly's body eased, and even Ariel's cries decreased into sniffles.

Maybe she'd been picking up on Carly's tension all along.

Now that Eli was back, maybe she could breathe again. Maybe—

He burst through the door, urgency in every motion…

And his face bruised and marred by dried blood.

* * *

"Eli!" Carly's frightened cry ignited Ariel's sniffles into screams.

He should have thought this through. Bursting through the door like a scene out of a horror movie wasn't good for anyone, but he'd been driven to know that Carly and Ariel and Lizzie and Reena were all safe. He'd forgotten his own injuries.

His hand went to his eyebrow, brushing across the crust of dried blood and trailing it down his face to his cheek. "I'm fine."

"You don't look fine." Carly approached, practiced eyes scanning his forehead and cheek. "What happened to you?" The words were remarkably calm, and her posture was studiously at ease. Either she was unaffected or she was working to calm Ariel, whose cries were dialing back into shuddering inhales.

Lizzie was watching him and judging his silence, he was sure. He'd talked to her on the phone earlier, so she knew everything that had happened. The last thing he wanted was her giving in to her controlling streak and spilling the details to Carly before he could. He longed to be with just Carly and Ariel, to decompress from the day and to know they were both truly safe.

That meant he'd have to take control and be a bit of a jerk about it. "Lizzie, Emmett wants you in Pueblo ASAP. Mia is our top priority." She truly was and they all knew it, but he was aware he didn't have to be so abrupt about it.

Lizzie's eyebrow went up and her head tilted in slight amusement, but then whatever she'd planned to say evaporated. "I'm on my way. If she's in Rolls's grandmother's house, we'll find her." She called to Reena and headed for the door before she turned back around. "Just pray she's in that house." Her eyes were sad yet determined. "Carly, it was nice to spend time with you." With a nod to Eli, she was gone.

He did pray, harder than he could remember praying, that Mia would be in that house and would be safe, that they could end this today and bring her home to her grandfather. He'd been praying off and on during the entire drive about Mia, Carly, Ariel…himself. His emotions were wrung out and his physical strength was almost gone.

In the wake of Lizzie's departure, the silence was loud, and it took a second for him to realize that Ariel's cries had stopped. The baby was sound asleep, breathing noisily in Carly's arms.

She carefully moved toward the pack-and-play, shooting Eli a glance. "I guess all it took was for you to come home."

Home. Was that what this was? He looked away as Carly settled Ariel and covered her with a light blanket. How long had it been since he'd felt at home? His farm was a house and some land and the place he liked most to be, but he couldn't say it was a home. It lacked something.

Something like laughter, love, the words of conversations big and small in the kitchen over dinner or on the porch over coffee.

Over the past few months, he'd talked to Carly more than he'd talked to anyone. How had he not realized that until now?

"So would you like to tell me why you look like a base-ball bat found your face?" Carly had straightened and stood in front of him before he realized she'd moved. She was eye-ing his forehead while her own wrinkled.

For the first time, he felt the pulse of a wound that reacted to every beat of his heart. He'd been so hopped-up on adren-aline and getting back to the cabin that he hadn't stopped to consider his own condition. "Do I have to?"

Narrowing her eyes, Carly nodded then pointed at the kitchen table. "Sit." When he started to argue that he'd be fine, she jammed her finger toward the table again. "Sit, please. I said the magic word, so you have to do it."

He offered a mock salute while he bit back a smile. She'd make a great mother for Ariel. She didn't take backtalk or argument. She was firm yet loving. He made his way to the table while she dug in the backpack she used as Ariel's diaper bag.

By the time he'd settled in a seat, she'd made her way to the pump in the kitchen. She came to the table with what appeared to be a clean cloth diaper, a package of wipes, a cup of water and a small first aid kit.

He eyed the assortment. "You are not cleaning my head with a diaper."

"Relax, prizefighter. It's never been used for its intended purpose. Wendy always used them as rags or cloths." She laid her things out on the table then twirled her finger. "Turn toward me. Let me get a look."

"I'm not a horse," he grumbled but obeyed. He didn't have a mirror, and he hadn't checked his appearance in the car, but he could imagine from the throbbing over his eye and his cheek and the itching of dried blood on his skin that he looked like something that had walked out of a horror movie.

"You'd be amazed how tending wounds crosses species. It's similar. I can even stitch you up if you have dental floss lying around."

Boy, he hoped it wouldn't come to that.

The smile in her words said it shouldn't, but he wasn't sure he should trust her. She was using her *keep-an-animal-calm* voice. He wasn't sure how he felt about that.

Her fingers were cool on his forehead as she ran them above his eyebrow, down his temple, and to his cheek.

The light touch did something in his stomach, clenching his muscles as though he hadn't eaten food in weeks. How long had it been since anyone had touched him? He'd comforted Carly earlier, sure, but that had been from a place of strength. He hadn't let a soul comfort him after Hailey and Ivy and Theo were killed. He'd shrugged off hugs and well-wishes. To be on the receiving end of someone's care slowly untangled knots he hadn't realized were tied up in his muscles, in his heart.

Carly didn't seem to notice the windstorm spinning inside him. Her practiced eye followed her fingers as they gently tested the tender places on his face.

He winced when she pressed a particularly sore spot on his cheek.

"Sorry if I hurt you." She muttered the words as though they were an afterthought. "I'm not used to talking to my patients." Stepping back, she grabbed the cloth diaper and dipped it into the water. "I'm going to wash off some of the blood, get a good look at the cut and make sure it doesn't look worse when it's clean. It's not bleeding, so I feel like it won't need stitches, but I'm not totally sure yet."

He wanted to crack a joke about how his great-grandmother used to cut "butterfly bandages" out of medical tape to avoid stitches, but his voice wouldn't work. It was as though her fingers had gripped him by the throat. He settled for a brief nod.

She was just about to touch his face with the water when panic alarms went off in his brain. She was standing too close. This was too much. He'd already talked more to her than any other woman since Hailey, and the last thing he wanted was to be feeling things in his chest because of her.

The chair scraped along the floor as he shoved it back

and stood. "I've got it. It's fine. If it starts bleeding, I'll let you know."

He grabbed the cloth from her hand and stalked to the pump in the kitchen, fighting the urge to grip the counter and stare out the window, wishing the cabin was bigger so he could hide.

Wishing he didn't feel like his heart might be splintering.

ELEVEN

Carly whipped toward the pack-and-play to make sure the chair's scraping hadn't awakened Ariel. She fought the urge to apologize to Eli, even though she had no idea what had happened.

Ariel slept on, her slight snuffles the only sound in the small cabin.

Eli stood by the pump built into the rough counter that passed for a kitchen, his shoulders rising and falling with each breath.

There were a thousand questions she wanted to ask, but she kept her mouth shut. She'd seen the panic in his expression, the sudden jolt that said this wasn't about physical pain. It was definitely emotional.

He didn't need her prying into his business. She'd done something to trigger him, and that was all that mattered. Her presence was the problem.

So she removed herself from his presence. Leaving the front door open, she walked out onto the porch to one of the weathered wooden rocking chairs that looked like they might fall apart if she breathed too hard. Settling down on the gray wood, she carefully avoided splinters and stared into the trees, the paw prints that Lizzie had mentioned earlier heavy on her mind.

Growing up with parents who were addicts and in foster care situations that occasionally turned volatile, she'd learned from a young age how to read people's emotions before they spoke, to look for what was behind their words and actions.

Eli's abrupt departure from the table was fear. It had flashed in his eyes, drowning out the warmth that had begun to brighten his gaze only moments before.

She wouldn't lie and say she hadn't felt it, too. Her patients were horses and cows and even a few llamas or alpacas. She didn't doctor humans, and certainly not men she felt attracted to.

She dropped her gaze to a clump of bushes at the edge of the clearing, finally admitting the truth to herself. She was drawn to Eli, and she had been since the first time she'd run into him jogging down the road in front of their houses. How could she not be? He was all rugged, redheaded, in-shape law enforcement officer, always out with Wrangler at his side on his jogs.

But when she'd spent time watching over Thunder, and Eli had stood watch alongside her, talking to her through the long hours of the night…

Well, a girl couldn't help but daydream, even if she'd eventually squashed those daydreams flat and refused to consider them any longer. She'd known from the start, every time they'd chatted at church or jogged together on the country roads or run into each other at KC's Coffee, that he had some sort of emotional baggage, something that held him back. He'd always talked about her, asked her questions, made her feel seen…but he'd rarely talked about himself.

Now that he'd told her he'd lost a wife and an unborn child, so much made sense. He'd known unimaginable grief. Pain she couldn't begin to fathom. He was wrestling with things he wasn't speaking about. But…

But he was drawn to her, too. She could see it and had ignored it as she was evaluating his injuries. It had been in his posture, his jaw, his eyes…

Until fear had flashed like lightning. Something about her terrified him.

It might just be that he'd felt something that he'd long ago packed away.

She shoved her foot against the worn wooden floor and set her chair to rocking. She had knowledge about his emotional state that he didn't realize she had. What did she do with it? It made this friendship feel off balance, as though she was keeping something from him.

If she was wrong, or if he didn't want to feel things for her, then bringing it up would only drive them apart.

Not that they were together, but she valued his friendship, and she wouldn't sacrifice it on the altar of speculation.

Something brushed in the doorway, then there was a footstep.

Eli appeared at her elbow.

When she looked up, he was looking down at her with a slightly sheepish expression on his face. "There's no mirror in there."

Not trusting her voice since he'd interrupted a pretty deep thought, she simply arched an eyebrow and hoped he wouldn't take her silence as anger.

He held up a couple of bandages. "I can't see to put them where they need to go."

There were a lot of things she could say. There were a lot of questions she could ask. None of them involved her getting into his personal space, not when her own emotions were rocking back and forth over a crush she'd thought she had managed to squelch. She swallowed everything personal, every deeper feeling she had for him, and shoved him squarely into the friend zone. Bracing her hands on the arms of the rocker, she stood. "Well, that does create a problem. Wouldn't want to get adhesive on the actual cut."

He winced, then passed her the bandages as she motioned for him to lean against the railing, which would bring his tall self a little bit closer to her eye level without her standing over him the way she had in the cabin. It created a little bit of distance, at least.

He complied. "I'm sorry about…" Eli waved his hand toward the cabin then braced it behind him on the railing.

Peeling the wrapper off the bandage, Carly stiffened her spine and prepared herself to step into his personal space. Before she peeled the adhesive from the back, she eyed the cut above his eye and a smaller one on his cheek. A bruise had formed around the points of impact, but the cuts didn't appear deep enough to need stitches. He'd managed to get some antibiotic ointment onto them, so she carefully positioned the bandage over his eye, making sure her fingers didn't touch skin.

Still, while she had him where he couldn't move…

She opened the second packet. "It's fine, what happened in there. I understand. You…you lost your wife, your child, your future." When he stiffened, she chose her next words carefully. There were suspicions racing through her head, and she cared enough to want to coax him to talk, something it seemed he might never have done before. She'd never been one to pull punches, and she wasn't going to start now. She'd seen too many friendships and families ruined over the unsaid. While she didn't want to dive into anything romantic, if they were truly friends, then she should be able to speak her mind about other things. "It's not disrespectful of you to keep living."

He was close enough that she could tell he stopped breathing. As if it took a herculean effort, he dragged his eyes from the cabin door to hers. His brown gaze held hers, searching, processing.

Would he pull away, or would he listen to what she had to say? Whether he was really feeling things for her or not, he needed to know he wasn't betraying his wife or his daughter. She bit down on her next words to give him a moment to think and pulled the backing off the next bandage before gently applying it to his cheek.

When she started to lower her arm, he grabbed her wrist gently. "What made you say that?" His voice was so low it barely qualified as a whisper.

"I honestly don't know." It had been a bold statement, but her history had made her bold in some respects, if not in others. There was no way she'd flat-out state that her heart was stirring toward him and had been for quite some time. That was too much. "I think you have friends, and I think we're friends. I think you hold parts of your life away from your friends as if they're somehow sacred." Maybe she should rephrase that. "They *are* sacred. Your memories and your marriage and your family…those things are beautiful and God gave them to you, but…" She wanted to look away, but those brown eyes held her in place. "Your story didn't end that day. A beautiful chapter closed in the worst possible way. It deserves for you to cherish it and love it and always hold it in a special place. But you're still breathing. You still have a purpose. You can't stop living. That would be the disrespectful thing."

His eyebrows drew together slightly, but not in the anger or the defensiveness she'd expected. Instead, he appeared to be thinking. "What made you say that?"

It was the same question again, and she still had no answer. "I don't—"

A soft sound cut her off and drew Eli's gaze down.

Carly started to step back, but his grip on her wrist tightened. "Don't move." The command was quiet but so firm it demanded she obey.

Her gaze slipped down as well.

At her feet, inches from her shoe, a massive rattlesnake slithered closer.

Lightning shot through Eli and jolted his heart into a painfully fast rhythm.

Every muscle in his body, every thought in his mind, screamed for him to shove Carly to safety and to run.

His grandfather's voice whispered above the shrieking fear. *Move slowly. Snakes are more afraid of you than you are of them.*

That had been easy to believe when he was eleven and there hadn't been an actual rattler inches away, flicking his tongue to sense his surroundings.

"Eli…" Carly's voice was weaker than the water in the creek behind the cabin. Her body was tensed like one of the trees surrounding them. He doubted she could move, even though she wanted to.

"Be still. He won't strike unless you scare him." Despite what most people feared, snakes weren't out to kill everything in their path.

Again, something that was easier to believe when there wasn't one in striking distance.

"I've seen what snakes can do to animals."

"When animals spook them." He exhaled slowly, trying to keep them both calm. "He won't strike unless he's threatened." Then what would he do? He'd been raised not to kill a creature unless the danger was clear or he needed food.

Just in case, he slipped his free hand to his pistol and wrapped his hand around the grip.

"Eli." Carly's voice shook, though it was only an exhale.

Her panic nearly ripped his heart out. The ache was more real than his own fear. "I've got you. I promise." A fierce protectiveness rose from somewhere behind his stomach. Carly and Ariel were his to protect. He would not fail them.

He kept his focus on the creature at his feet. The snake was at least three feet long and as big around as his wrist. The pointed head was unmistakable, as was the massive set of rattles. The diamond pattern of his skin would have been a thing of beauty if there was a wall of glass separating them.

Instead, the snake paused a mere inch away, a dealer of death. If he struck, they were so far from help. What if the snake struck them both? What if—

He inhaled deeply. If he panicked, Carly would panic. If they both panicked, he had no doubt that one or both of them would be goners.

"Ariel. She's inside." Carly's breaths stuttered. "I have to—"

"The snake is out here. She's safe. They don't travel in packs." At least not that he'd ever heard of. *Lord, get us out of this without anyone getting hurt. Please.*

The rattler's tongue nearly brushed Carly's bare foot. She whimpered and wavered on her feet.

Eli gripped her wrist tighter and prepared to draw his pistol if the rattler so much as hinted he was going to strike.

The snake turned his attention to Eli's boot, apparently decided it was safer, and slithered closer, up and over the toe. His weight was enough for Eli to feel it through the thick leather. The sensation seemed to crawl up his leg and into his spine as the rattler slithered over his foot, wriggling back and forth.

The tail rattled softly as it dropped to the floor and the snake continued on its way, disappearing into the leaves off the side of the porch.

Carly whimpered again, and her knees buckled. Eli barely caught her before she dropped. He was fairly certain his own legs wouldn't have held him up if he wasn't leaning against the railing. Pulling her to him, he held her close as she shuddered, though she didn't cry as he'd thought she might.

Instead she quaked against him, drawing breath after shaky breath. "I think I might be sick."

She could join the club. As the adrenaline ebbed, his stomach rolled. He needed to not let her know how much that had shaken him though. "It's okay. He's gone."

"But not far." She pulled out of his arms and turned toward the door, walking as she spoke. "I can't have Ariel here if—"

"It's fine." He grabbed her hand before she could get too far. "Really." He hoped he sounded convincing, because he had nowhere else to take the two of them. He was far more concerned about the danger from men than he was about forest creatures…even slithering ones.

He tried hard not to shudder.

She stopped, half turned toward him, then slowly extracted her fingers from his grasp. "I…" She rubbed her temples. "I have a ripping headache now."

"Adrenaline crash." He wasn't going to admit that his head was aching, too, though that was more likely from being smashed into his SUV's rear window. "Go rest. I'll listen out for Ariel, and I promise to stay right by the door so that nothing can come in." There were certainly enough cracks in the old cabin to allow a snake in by some other route, but he wasn't about to say that out loud.

For a second, she eyed him with suspicion, then she pivoted and walked inside.

He turned away to keep himself from watching her go. Her earlier questions had shaken him more than he cared to admit. Why would she ask him almost the same things as Emmett, only a couple of hours apart? They'd used almost the exact same words, too.

Why would those questions come just before and just after he'd allowed himself a brief blip of feeling something for Carly?

He braced his hands against the railing and stared into the trees. Life had been so much simpler when he was out here as a kid with his grandfather. If he could warn that kid of what was to come, would he?

He wrapped his fingers around the porch railing, ignoring the splinters that poked his skin. Was Carly right? Was Emmett? Was it disrespectful of him to live like he'd died, too?

His grandfather would likely say yes.

His eyes slipped closed. Hailey would definitely say yes. She'd loved him fiercely and completely, and if she knew he'd basically become a hermit since she passed away, she'd read him the riot act.

Hailey was his wife and always would be. Was there room in his heart for another woman…or another child?

The sun slipped to the west, lengthening the shadows as he prayed and thought and wished for the first time that he had someone to talk to. He'd even settle for his grandfather's friend Isaac right now, although the man wasn't big on words or emotions. It was odd that he hadn't come by to check on the cabin in the past day or so, especially given all the activity. If he was busy hunting, he might have ranged away from his cabin, which was nearly two miles away and even more remote than this one. His off-the-grid lifestyle kept him busy and—

Eli's phone buzzed, and his heart picked up speed when Lizzie's number lit the screen.

News. Please, Lord, let them have found Mia. Please. This could all be over. The ring could be stopped. Mia and her unborn daughter could be safe. He stepped off the porch and onto the slick pine straw, watching for slithering snakes as he pulled the phone to his ear. "Tell me they were there."

The silence was heavy and dragged his heart to his feet. What if they were too late? What if—

"The place was empty."

Lizzie's statement hollowed out his chest. *Empty.* He hadn't realized he'd been carrying such subconscious high hopes. His attack and Carly's presence and the snake had driven away everything else but, deep inside, his heart had been primed for relief. "Did you guys find anything at all?"

Road noise filled the space. Lizzie was in the car, probably driving back toward HQ in Denver. "It's almost worse than finding nothing." She sniffed. "We missed them. They were there. Crime scene techs are sweeping Rolls's grandmother's house for clues, but I don't know that they'll find anything more."

"How do you know?" The gutting was complete. Mia had been there, probably on the edge of rescue, and someone had swept her away.

"We found a thin gold bracelet on the back stoop, caught between two bricks. It had an *M* charm on it. I sent a photo to Emmett, who checked with Dodger, and he confirmed it's a bracelet that he and Mia's grandmother bought for her several years ago. She wears it all the time, never takes it off."

He sank onto the porch step. "How's Dodger?" Mia's

grandfather had to be heartsick. To know they'd been so close…

"Quiet. He didn't have much to say."

Neither did Eli, if he was being honest. "Derek Rolls knows we're onto him. This is at least proof we're moving in the right direction, but he's going to move her somewhere that's harder to find." Had the man seen him talking to his ex-wife? Had the assault in the parking lot been about Carly as he'd suspected, or had it been about silencing him before he could pass along the intel he'd learned from Gwen Marker?

"I do have one bit of good news."

"I'll take anything." Right now, every part of his life felt upended, from the search for Mia to discovering who was trying to take Ariel to these feelings that Carly was stirring inside him.

"Emmett wants you and me to head into Oak City first thing tomorrow to pull surveillance on a free clinic. A staff member reported a dark-colored van sitting nearby for the past couple of days. The people in it never get out. They called Oak City PD, who passed it along to us rather than stepping in."

"Okay." It was something to hang their hopes on, but it also meant leaving Ariel and Carly behind again, and he was pretty sure there was no one else on the task force who could step in this time. Did he dare take her with him? Did he—

Ariel squawked and Eli rocketed to his feet. If Carly was asleep, he didn't want the child to wake her. "Text me details." He ended the call and crept inside.

Carly was sound asleep on the cot, her face slack and peaceful. He watched her breathe for a few minutes, allowing himself to feel the tug at his heart before Ariel squeaked again. When he looked down, she was on her back in the pack-and-play, grabbing her toes and releasing them. When she caught sight of Eli, her brow furrowed, but then she squeaked again and held her hands out to him, opening and closing her fingers.

Did he dare pick her up? Did he remember how? It had been years since he'd held his niece, and he'd had no desire to pick up an infant since—

Ariel blew a raspberry at him, still reaching up.

He could do this. He had to.

Bending at the waist, he cradled her head and lifted her to his chest. Her warm, chubby body curled into his. Far from breaking his heart or dragging him backward into *what might have been*, she warmed something inside him, dragging out a smile as she snuggled close.

But then her chubby fingers latched onto his lip and pulled. Hard. The instant pain brought the sting of tears, but he ignored them. She was kind of cute, so he'd forgive her.

"Come on," he whispered to Ariel as he stepped onto the porch. "Let's go see the outside world so Carly can sleep."

He scanned the small yard for danger and found none. Walking down the steps, he turned Ariel toward the world, cradling her back against his chest. His heart ached at the thought of what might have been, but not in the way he'd expected.

Yes, it was bittersweet, but it lacked the crushing grief he'd felt for so long.

For the first time in a very long time, Eli felt hope…like he might truly survive.

TWELVE

Standing at the window, Carly watched Eli walk around the small yard, letting Ariel touch pine tree bark and picking up rocks then holding them up for her to feel.

He was way more of a natural at parenting than she was. While she panicked sometimes and worried about doing everything wrong, there was Eli, helping Ariel safely explore the world.

He'd have been a great father to his child.

Her heart seized, aching for his grief. How was he able to smile at Ariel when his heart had to be breaking?

She should step in, but it was kind of nice to let someone else carry the load for a moment. She'd hardly had time to breathe, let alone to process all the changes in her life. Now—

Eli turned and caught her watching. He smiled bigger, then lifted Ariel's hand to wave at her.

Now her breath caught for a whole different reason. He looked relaxed, maybe even happy. There was a new joy in his eyes that hadn't been there even an hour earlier when she'd walked inside to rest.

Maybe God was answering prayers. She'd sure prayed enough on his behalf over the past day or so.

Stepping outside, she called to them. "Is she going to be a biologist now? Study trees? Rocks? No snakes, please."

She shuddered and looked at her feet, just to be sure the behemoth hadn't returned. It was shocking she'd slept without feeling a thousand wriggly things slithering all over her skin.

At the sound of her voice, Ariel's head snapped up and she babbled a string of nonsense syllables, reaching toward the porch.

"Guess I've been cast aside." Eli carried Ariel over and passed her up from his spot on the ground. "She's been exploring the world, safely up here away from any friends who might come crawling by. I was careful."

"I believe you." She rocked Ariel from side to side as the baby wrapped her fingers in Carly's brown hair and tugged. Rather than disentangle the strands, she studied Eli, who was watching Ariel.

He seemed to be at peace, and he was looking at the baby more than he had the entire time they'd been together.

Carly cleared her throat. "Are you…okay?"

Eli's eyes shifted to hers, though nothing else about him moved. He watched her for a minute. "Better than I thought I'd be." He inhaled so heavily that his shoulders lifted. "While we've been out here exploring, I've been thinking about what you said." He looked at Ariel and ran a finger down the tiny arm that was winding deeper into Carly's hair. "Living isn't betraying anyone." He stepped onto the porch and sat down in one of the rocking chairs behind her. The wood creaked in a way that was almost soothing.

She resumed her seat, rocking gently as Ariel shoved a fistful of Carly's hair into her mouth.

"I had a daughter I never got to hold." Eli rocked slowly, staring into the trees. "She'd have been three now. The crash was so violent, the fire afterward so—" The words choked off, and he turned away. "I never even got to know what she looked like. She was moments from being born, and I lost her and her mother and my closest friend all in the same instant."

Carly's eyes slipped shut, the pain in his voice so raw she could hardly stand to hear it.

Wrangler walked out of the house and leaned against Eli's leg, likely sensing the anguish in Eli's tone.

"For the first fifteen months, I had horrific, graphic night-mares. I took a leave of absence from the PD. I saw a counselor. I managed to get past that part, but the guilt and the grief…" He took a deep breath. "We had a place outside of town, and I wasn't there when Hailey went into labor. I was working a case on the other side of the city, and our next-door neighbor, who was my closest friend, was driving her to the hospital. I was going to meet them there. Maybe if I'd been driving…" The silence spoke more to his regret than words ever could.

The urge to tell him no, that he'd probably be dead, was strong. She sensed this was sacred ground, that he was speaking things he'd rarely spoken, so she kept silent to keep from bursting the bubble he was in.

"I'd been lead in taking down a drug ring the year before, and the kingpin was angry. He thought I was driving my SUV and he…" His fingers dug into the arm of the chair. "He shot Theo through the front window. The car flipped and caught on fire. He thought Theo was me. He died in my place, with Hailey and Ivy."

"Eli…" She'd be shocked if he'd heard her. The story had ripped her breath away.

As though sensing both of their pain, Ariel stilled and snuggled into her chest, curling into a ball.

"Don't. I don't need sympathy. I need…" The rocking chair creaked in the stretched silence. "You and my task force leader, Emmett, both said similar things today, and you're both right. I've been hanging on to grief like it's an oxygen tank or something, like if I let myself heal it will… Like it will somehow say that Hailey and Ivy don't mean anything."

"They'll always mean something."

"I know. At least, I'm learning." He smiled in Ariel's direction, and she let loose with a string of baby babble that made a smile reach his eyes. "I've been afraid I'd be betraying them, but you're both right. Living isn't a betrayal. It's honoring them." His gaze slid from Ariel to her. "And maybe I can actually admit that—"

His phone buzzed, the sound harsh as it popped the bubble they'd been sitting in. He held her gaze, a promise she couldn't quite understand in his expression. "I'm sorry. I have to—" At her nod, he answered the call and started to speak.

She tuned him out, burying her face in Ariel's neck. What would he have said if that call hadn't come in? Was he also feeling something deeper than either of them were free to admit? He'd become a friend over the months they'd known each other, but he was opening up to her more now than he ever had before. It had to be hard for him, and he'd chosen her to share with. Did that mean he might—

"Carly?" He was leaning into the space between their chairs, the phone extended. "It's Eva. She has news about who might be trying to take Ariel."

Reflexively, her arms squeezed around the infant, eliciting a squawk and a wriggle of protest.

"Was that her?" A voice Carly recognized as Eli's technical person, Eva, came through the phone's speaker. "If this was any other day, I'd ask for a video call."

Sadly, it wasn't any other day. Carly loosened her hold on the baby, though she wanted to hang on tighter. "What have you found, Eva?"

"Well, first of all, there's been a formal petition filed for guardianship. A guy named Les Cassel, who used to be a cop at Oak City, is named on the doc. Does that ring a bell?"

She'd only briefly met a few of Mike's fellow police officers, and she'd rarely heard him speak of them. He didn't talk much about the job at home. "No. Who is he?"

"I'm digging into his background now. He was on the department until about six months ago, then he resigned and went to work for a home restoration company as a foreman. That and a picture are all I have so far. I've sent a text to Eli with his photo along with a photo of the attorney listed on the petition, a guy named Dominic Gunther. He's not the most ethical guy. He used to work for the DA's office, but he got into some shady dealings a few years ago and was let go. He's had several complaints filed against him for various violations, and he's come close to being disbarred. He tends to work with a rough crowd. I've put a call in to his office, but I can promise you he won't get back to me."

"I actually know that name." Eli drew the phone closer to himself. "I was only at Oak City for a few weeks before his name crossed my desk. I've never met him, but he's well known for skating the edge of the law. Every cop at OCPD knows his name. Think we should send someone over for a face-to-face with him?"

"Would it do any good? He won't talk without a warrant. But have Carly look at those pictures. You, too. See if either of them looks familiar."

A lump in Carly's throat made it hard to speak. When Eli held the phone up, she leaned closer, then shook her head at the photo of a generic looking man in a suit, probably the attorney.

Eli swiped to the next photo. It was a standard police portrait of a clean-cut officer in front of a flag, his brown hair cut short and his brown eyes staring straight into the camera. "I don't know about that one. It could be him, but the man at my house was bald and was bigger. Maybe? I don't know for sure. I'm sorry." Her voice cracked as she sat back, away from the photo of the man who might be trying to steal Ariel. "What if the paperwork is real? What happens then?"

"Nothing." Eva's voice was calm and reassuring. "Guardianship of Ariel automatically went to your friend Wendy on Mike's death. Wendy was her birth mother, and her will would be the one that stands. It clearly names you as Ariel's guardian. These papers, which are likely fake, would have become null on Mike's death even if they were real, because he ceased to be Ariel's guardian. I guess whoever is behind this wasn't smart enough to change both wills."

"Unless there's another one floating around with Wendy's name on it." Her biggest fears raised their rabid heads. She could lose Ariel to violent, greedy men who—

"Not that I've found." Eva's voice was quiet. "I'd imagine these guys want to gain access to that safe deposit box and that crypto account and that's it."

"And then what?" That was the thing that scared her most. What would happen to Ariel if they somehow managed to get custody? After they had what they wanted, what would they do with her?

"Eva, I'll call you back." Eli ended the call, cutting off Eva as she was about to say something, and laid a hand on Carly's arm. "Nothing is going to happen to either of you. We have names. We'll make this work. I'll call the chief at Oak City and—"

"No." She stood, pulling away from him. Didn't he understand? There were corrupt cops in Oak City. Couldn't he see it?

Eli rose with her and stepped into her personal space. "Carly, I work there. I know these guys. I know cops. Just like any other profession, there are one or two bad seeds. That's true everywhere. But I promise you, the chief is above-board, as is the vast majority of the rest of the department. While I appreciate and understand your concern, I'll be careful. I do think the chief needs to be aware that a former officer is trying to use the courts to kidnap Ariel."

Fear went to war with common sense. She trusted Eli. He wouldn't lie to her.

But she'd also thought that Mike and Wendy were trustworthy. Everything she'd learned said that Mike hadn't been the husband and father she'd thought he was. "Okay." What other choice did she have? Eli was going to make that call whether she agreed to it or not. He had to.

He lifted his phone and moved to press the screen, but suddenly he stopped and snapped toward the right. Wrangler stood and growled low as Eli reached for his pistol. "Carly, get inside. Now."

She backed toward the door, her insides quaking, as a man stepped out of the trees carrying a rifle.

Eli's grip tightened on his pistol as a man stepped out of the darkening shadows, a rifle hanging over his arm.

When Carly and Ariel were safely behind closed doors, Eli pulled the pistol from its holster. "Federal agent! Put down the weapon and show me your hands!"

The shadowy figure stopped moving. "Are you serious right now, Eli?"

His muscles relaxed so quickly that he nearly dropped his weapon. The air left his lungs in a soft whoosh. "Isaac." He holstered his sidearm and walked down the two steps to greet the older man with a quick, back-slapping hug. "What are you doing sneaking around? If it had been any darker, this might have ended badly for us both."

"For you, maybe. I'm fast for an old man." His grandfather's closest friend was broad-shouldered and athletic, even in his seventies. A thick, trimmed gray beard covered the lower half of Isaac's face, and his hair was still cut to regulation, even though he spent the majority of his time alone in a cabin a couple of miles away, off the grid. He was clearly none the worse for wear. "I came to check on the place like I do every week. Didn't know you were here until I saw the vehicle." He jerked his chin toward the cabin. "Who's the woman and baby? And who whacked you in the face with a two-by-four?"

He gave Isaac a quick rundown of the past couple of days. He'd nearly forgotten his injury with all that had happened since, but just talking about it made the skin under the bandages pulse with each heartbeat.

It also reminded him that he had duties away from the cabin, out in the real world.

Maybe Isaac was an answer to prayer. "I need a favor."

The older man arched a silvery-gray eyebrow over steel blue eyes. "Wow. I don't see you for years then you immediately ask me for something?" A smile took the sting out of the words. "You know I've got your back, just like I had your grandfather's. What do you need?"

"Someone to watch over Carly and Ariel for a few hours in the morning while I—"

"Nope." Isaac physically recoiled, taking a step back toward the woods. His forehead creased. "Can't do that."

Eli's head jerked with the shock of the abrupt denial. He'd always known Isaac to be a loner, but he'd always been kind. The harshness of his demeanor cracked like a whip and stung just as painfully.

The burn hit Eli in the heart, robbing him of the joy and freedom he'd built up in the past few hours. He was ripped between his promise to protect the little family in the cabin and his duty to find a killer and rescue Mia. He couldn't do both.

He was failing at both.

His shoulders slumped.

A soft shuffle lifted his head. Isaac had stepped back into the clearing, standing on the edge where the shadows were deepest. His face was shielded by darkness. "It's tough to be a cop."

Eli turned his face away. If Isaac wasn't going to help him, he didn't want to chat.

With a long sigh, Isaac spoke again. "It's also tough to lose your family."

He wasn't surprised Isaac knew his story, even though they hadn't seen each other in four years.

His grandfather had died six years earlier, felled by a lightning-fast heart attack, but clearly his family had been talking.

Isaac seemed to read his mind. "I might not see you as often as I once did, and I might not be on the internet or have a satellite dish, but I do manage to get news. And I do keep up with your parents. They fill me in on how the family is doing. So yeah, I know what happened." Isaac shifted the rifle, letting the barrel point straight down by his feet. "You and I are more alike than you think."

He'd never heard Isaac's story. As a child, he'd always assumed the man lived like this because he wanted to. He'd never considered that something might have driven him into seclusion. Had he lost someone? A wife? A child? Both?

From the cabin, Ariel set up a wail that sounded like her hungry cry.

Both men looked toward the sound, and when he turned back to Isaac, the older man's expression was pained.

They couldn't talk about the thing that hung in the air between them. Eli needed to unload the supplies he'd nearly forgotten he'd brought with him. They were all hungry, and he should set up the bouncer so Ariel could have a safe place besides the pack-and-play.

One problem remained. "I need your help, Isaac. Please. I can't leave them here alone, and I can't take them into town with me. This case I'm working, it's life or death for a young woman who's pregnant." There wasn't time to go into every detail.

Isaac blinked twice, then turned to walk away. "I'll be back at sunup." He disappeared into the shadows like something was chasing him as Ariel's cries filled the clearing.

Eli watched until he couldn't see his grandfather's friend any longer, then trudged to the SUV. He was relieved for the backup, but guilt hovered, too. What would this favor cost Isaac?

THIRTEEN

Eli stretched and held his hands over his head, trying not to groan in the front seat of his unmarked SUV. Sleep had been elusive the previous night. Emotions had wrung him out like a wet rag. Thoughts refused to stop racing around his head like horses at Churchill Downs. Between this case and the danger surrounding Carly and Ariel, he was running on adrenaline and prayer.

He'd doubted Isaac would show, but the man had appeared at sunrise and taken a seat in a porch rocker, refusing to step inside the cabin. As long as he was watching over Carly and Ariel, did it matter where he sat?

Eli took a long draw on the massive to-go cup he'd picked up on his way to meet Lizzie on the outskirts of Oak City.

"Coffee is the last thing you need." From the passenger seat, Lizzie looked at him over the rim of her own travel mug.

"Hypocrite."

She smiled. "It's tea. And I'm not the one bouncing their leg so hard that the whole SUV is an earthquake zone."

Hmm. He hadn't even realized he was doing that. He purposely sat still, eyeing the front of the clinic that Emmett had asked them to surveil. In the rear of the SUV, Wrangler and Reena were curled up and resting, waiting for orders.

Surveillance was mind-numbing, and it was quiet enough

in the SUV to take a nap. It was going to take a lot to maintain his focus and to keep his eyes open. He'd never struggled this hard.

Sitting up taller in the seat, he watched the parking lot for the dark van that had reportedly been lurking there the past few days. "We're doing this for Mia." He said it out loud, needing to ground himself in the moment. The search for Mia and her unborn child was never far from his mind. She needed rescue, and their task force was her best hope.

"Yes." Lizzie sipped her tea then clicked the lid closed. "Maybe that van will show up and we'll put an end to this nightmare for Mia, Dodger and their family."

He hoped with all of his heart that would happen. "We need end this before they take another young woman." It was his worst fear. Every time his phone buzzed, his heart seized, terrified it was news of another abduction.

He surveyed the front of the clinic. Located in an older section of Oak City a few blocks from the courthouse, the low brick building had been built in the seventies and had housed government offices before the city consolidated into the courthouse in the early nineties.

A nonprofit had bought the building from the city and converted the space into medical offices for pregnant women who couldn't afford health care. Doctors and interns from local colleges staffed the place pro bono. They also offered counseling for young parents who either opted to raise their children or to place them for adoption through another arm of the nonprofit.

While the exterior of the building was faded, he knew from prior visits that the interior was clean, warm and welcoming. It was a wonderful endeavor, but it was also the perfect place for Derek Rolls and his lackeys to hunt for prey.

"Well, one of two things is happening." Lizzie looked over

her shoulder at the K-9s then back to the clinic's parking lot, which was two buildings away. "Either someone is illegally parking there to avoid paying for a spot closer to the court-house, or we're on to Rolls and his associates."

Lord, don't let this be a waste of time. Let us find those guys before they harm anyone else. Somehow, it felt like he could atone for what had happened to Hailey and Ivy if he could stop the baby-smuggling ring from killing again.

"So." Lizzie settled in and kept her eyes glued on the clinic. "Let's talk about you and Carly."

"I… What?" The shift in conversation jerked his head toward her, his eyebrow arching in question. How did she know there was something happening with Carly? "What did she say?"

Whoa. Had he just asked that question instead of spitting out the denial he'd planned?

Lizzie actually laughed. "Ah. So you want to know what she's saying when you aren't around, huh? Are you curious?"

More than he'd ever been curious about anything. His heart jolted at the thought of getting insight into what she might think of him. "I mean—"

"Hold that thought." Lizzie settled her tea into a cupholder and pointed. "I think our friends just showed up."

Sure enough, a dark blue van slipped into a space next to the only other car in the parking lot, an older gray sedan. The van appeared to be an old work vehicle that had been hap-hazardly painted a different color. Though the vehicle was shadowed, it was clear that two people sat inside. Whether it was two men or two women was tough to say.

Eli reached for his radio to call in the sighting but, before he could, a young woman stepped out of the clinic. She was heavily pregnant and looked almost like Hailey had in the last weeks of her pregnancy. She had that same wobble to her walk, and she'd rested her hand on her stomach as she exited the building into the July day. He winced for her, remembering Hailey's complaints about how the heat was ten times worse when she'd been carrying Ivy.

Shaking off the memories, he reached for the ignition as Lizzie took photos of the scene.

The young woman headed for the gray sedan, not seeming to pay any attention to the van. Eli's gut said this was not going to end well.

He started the SUV and put it into gear, ready to roll onto the scene. More than anything, his mind strained to yell for the young woman to protect herself, because if they were right—

The passenger door of the van opened, and a man stepped out. He was tall and thin with unkempt dark blond hair, just as Gwen Marker had described. "This might be Benny."

"Roll up to the street like you're leaving. If they snag her, we want to be moving."

Keeping an eye on the scene, Eli coasted to the parking lot entrance and onto the street as the maybe-Benny approached the girl. They chatted for a moment, then he walked toward the car with her. When they reached the vehicle, the man suddenly grabbed her and dragged her toward the opposite side of the van.

"Go!" Lizzie's shout echoed off the inside of the SUV.

In the back, the dogs scrambled up and barely kept their footing as Eli gunned the engine and roared the short distance to the clinic's parking lot. He slammed on the brakes, blocking the van in, and they both leaped out of the vehicle as he pressed the button to open the rear of the SUV. "Wrangler! *Stellen! Stellen!*"

The man froze, staring at Eli and Lizzie with empty blue eyes that matched Gwen's description of Benny.

The young woman screamed, struggling against the man's hold.

Eli and Lizzie drew their weapons, and Lizzie shouted, "Federal agents! Let her go and put your hands up!"

Before the man could comply, Wrangler raced forward and leaped, latching onto the man's arm.

He howled and released the young woman, who scrambled to keep her footing. She braced her hand on the van, regained her balance, and raced toward Lizzie.

Eli kept his focus on the man, who was wrestling with Wrangler and howling in pain. The maybe-Benny leaped toward the van, but the vehicle suddenly reversed, sliding off the parking lot into the dirt and gravel behind it. It narrowly grazed a tree as it skirted Eli's vehicle before it raced out of the lot and up the street.

Behind him, he heard Lizzie comfort the girl as she called in the van's description and location.

He kept his gun raised as he approached the man, then commanded Wrangler to release. "Wrangler. *Los.*"

The K-9 immediately let go, but he stood close, baring his teeth at the man who couldn't decide if he should watch Wrangler or Eli.

"Raise your hands slowly and get on your knees, or I let him take another shot at you." Eli approached slowly. "And if you're thinking of making a run for it, trust me, he's a lot faster than you are."

The terrified man's hands shot into the air, his arms shaking. "Okay. Okay."

Quickly, Eli handcuffed the man then commanded Wrangler to sit. "Looks like your partner took off without you."

Now that Wrangler had stood down, the man was defiant. He looked like he wanted to spit at Eli, but he turned his head away and stared at the trees, his posture rigid.

Guess he was opting for the tough-guy approach. "You don't have to talk. My partner has backup on the way to take you in, and you're going to want to chat with them, because we have your kidnapping attempt on video. For now, we can wait quietly for them… Benny."

The man flinched and flicked his gaze to Eli with a tinge of fear before his expression hardened and he looked away again. He didn't speak, even when an Oak City officer arrived to escort him to a holding cell.

It didn't matter. Eli was certain they'd found Benny. When he walked over to Lizzie, she was crouched before the young woman, who was sitting in a folding chair someone had brought outside.

Lizzie looked up when Eli approached then rested her hand on the girl's arm. "Eli, this is Sarah. Sarah, this is my team member Eli and his partner, Wrangler."

Sarah offered a shaky smile. "Wrangler looks like my uncle's dog."

As if he knew he was needed, Wrangler approached the girl, nosed at her knee, then rested his head on her leg.

This time, Sarah's smile was genuine. She looked down at the K-9 as she stroked his ears.

Lizzie turned her attention to the young woman. "You were telling me that you felt like someone was watching you?"

Nodding, Sarah kept her attention on Wrangler. "I thought it was just pregnancy hormones, you know?" Her other hand went to her stomach.

Eli's own stomach clenched at the protective gesture he'd often seen Hailey make, but the pain rolled past then ebbed. "Was there anything else strange?"

Sarah twisted her lips as she thought, then suddenly looked up at Lizzie. "Yesterday, I was working behind the counter at the grocery store. A guy came in. I'd seen him before. He's always nice, dressed really well. Asked me if I'd be interested in a program for young mothers, because he thought I could use some help since I was working so hard. I thought about it for a minute, but we were busy, and I didn't really give him an answer."

Eli caught Lizzie's quick glance. Could it be Derek Rolls? Were they closer than they'd thought? Lizzie followed up. "Can you describe him?"

"Light brown hair. Dressed like a businessman. Maybe thirty or forty?" She shook her head. "I really didn't look that close. He was just…average."

"Glasses?" Eli asked gently, afraid to spook her. "Tattoos? Birthmarks?"

"No." She chewed her lower lip. "But he maybe had brown or green eyes?"

It wasn't Derek Rolls, but it was possible they'd uncovered another player…or perhaps the kingpin.

They'd taken two steps back with the failed raid at the house, but maybe they were moving forward again. He thanked God they'd been in place to protect Sarah, but this was only one young woman.

What if they failed to save the next one?

Carly laid a sleeping Ariel in the pack-and-play, then cleaned up the smeared carrots from the table, her ears straining for Eli's arrival. It was late, and the sun had already set. He'd been gone all day, and that quiet man, Isaac, had simply sat on the porch with a rifle at his side like an old-timer in a Western movie.

She'd invited him in and had offered him a sandwich from the food Eli had brought the day before, but the older man had refused politely and maintained his post.

She sort of couldn't blame him about the sandwich, though. She'd turn cartwheels down Main Street for some hot food, but that wasn't likely to happen in the near future. She'd have to be content with more PB and J. She was grateful, but she was also hungry, and it was getting late.

While it was comforting to have Isaac there, his silence was disconcerting. The only time Isaac left his post was if Ariel cried or babbled. At those times, he'd step out into the yard and take a lap around the clearing, watching.

It was as though Ariel's presence upended him. Carly had to wonder why.

Instead of focusing on the silent stranger, she'd spent her day distracting herself with the treasure haul that Eli had purchased the day before. She hadn't had time to go through everything he'd brought until this morning, and she was awed by it all. They could stay here for weeks on the food, clothing and toys he'd purchased. There was so much extra, so much beyond what they could ever use… It was as though he'd made the purchases with both his head and his heart.

She wasn't certain how to think about that. Eli was a confusing man, one who was working through grief she couldn't fathom, even as she sorted through her own fresh pain.

Were they answers to one another's prayers? Or were they destined for heartbreak if they tried to begin something when they were both so broken?

The porch creaked as Isaac stood, and the sound of a vehicle approached.

Carly stood frozen in the center of the cabin before she recognized the engine. Eli was finally back.

She hadn't realized how concerned she'd been for him until she knew he was safe.

The doors to the SUV shut soon after the engine died,

and there was the low murmur of male conversation before Eli entered the cabin , carrying a small soft-sided cooler.

Wrangler trailed him and settled onto his bed as though he was as weary as the humans around him.

Crossing to the table, Eli set the cooler on it. "I know it's late, but I thought you might like something hot for dinner so I stopped for burgers. Isaac headed back to his cabin, so there's an extra, if you want to split it. They won't be much past lukewarm at this point, but it seemed like—"

She rushed him with a hug of gratitude, throwing herself into his arms. How had he known? "Thank you. For everything." For the protection, the food, the overwhelming amount of gifts and gear for Ariel… There was too much on her heart.

Eli froze, but then his arms slowly slipped around her waist, tentative, as though he was testing the waters. After a brief hesitation he drew her closer, tightening his hold as though he actually wanted to be near her.

He'd held her close as she'd cried, but this was different. This was by choice, and it sent a zing through Carly's stomach that went way beyond comfort, throwing wide open the doors to hidden places where she'd buried her attraction.

It was also a feeling of safety, of comfort, that she'd never felt before in her life. She dipped her head slightly, letting her forehead nestle into the space at the base of his neck, her heart hitching when his breath caught.

He felt it, too.

What did she do about it? Did she back away as if she wasn't drawn to him, as if she hadn't been drawn to him for months? Or did she—

His arms tightened around her. His chin dipped, brushing her temple. Was it a silent invitation?

Carly backed away slightly, their faces only inches apart

when her eyes caught his. There was a pause, as though the world held its breath, and then her heart decided for her. She brushed her lips across his, her heart aching for more.

But she really shouldn't. They were both bruised, broken. No matter how badly she wanted to pursue this, she couldn't push him toward something he might not be ready to chase with her.

Straightening her shoulders, she withdrew her arms from his neck and backed away, dragging her hands through her hair as she turned toward the table. She cleared her throat. "So, yeah. Thank you, because I was just really wishing for real food. Not that I'm not grateful for the sandwiches." She busied herself unpacking the bag, babbling in panic and embarrassment. "I'm grateful for everything. Thank you. Really."

Eli was silent.

When she'd set all of the food out on the table, including chips instead of fries, which would have been completely soggy—he'd thought of everything—she turned to see if he was still in the room.

He stood where she'd left him, watching her with an expression that was half fear, half wonder.

When her eyes caught his, his brow furrowed as though he'd never seen anything like her before and was trying to puzzle her out. Before she could address the strange air in the room, he shook his head and smiled. "I guess you, uhm, really were tired of peanut butter and jelly." He forced a laugh and pulled out the chair on the other side of the table. "I mean, there's also canned spaghetti and meatballs you could have eaten."

Carly slid into the chair across from him. She'd messed up so bad, had made this budding friendship so awkward by letting the pull to him get too strong. She never should have literally thrown herself at him. "Look…" Grabbing a napkin, she shredded the edges of it in her lap, reluctant to look him in the eye. "I'm sorry. You've got a lot to deal with and—"

"I'm not." The words were quiet, just above a whisper. They held hope and, possibly, a promise. "Carly, look at me."

Keeping her chin tucked, she lifted her eyes. Eli was watching her, the space across the table seeming to shrink. He simply offered a slow smile. "Eat before it gets any colder."

She squashed the small shimmer of disappointment at his reluctance to say more. They both needed time to heal. As much as she wished things could be different, she wasn't going to go all drama queen and demand he speak his mind.

Instead, she focused on the burger in front of her which was, amazingly, still better than lukewarm even after the forty-five-minute trip to her. She swallowed the first bite, which nearly brought her to tears. "It's perfect. Thank you." She swiped her mouth with a napkin. "I honestly can't remember the last time I ate real food, but it was days ago, before Wendy—"

"I understand."

There was no doubt he did. She ate half of the burger before she felt the need to break the silence. "How did it go today? Did you catch the guy who's taking those young women?"

"No." Eli studied the last third of his burger, which he had yet to put down. "But we made some headway. We did take one suspect into custody, and we prevented them from kidnapping another victim." He ran down a skeletal summary of his day, making it sound very clean and simple when she was certain it had been messy and complicated…and dangerous. "We're getting the security footage from the grocery store to see if we can get a good look at this guy on camera. If we can, then we have a fair shot of finding out who he is."

"And maybe where he's holding your friend's granddaughter." She'd prayed for the girl, Mia, off and on all day, letting her own grief fuel her petitions.

"I hope so."

They finished their burgers, chips and water while letting the conversation flow more easily, neither of them willing to circle back to the moment when her lips had touched his. It seemed something better forgotten.

When Ariel woke up while they were still talking an hour later, Eli started gathering the trash while Carly changed a diaper and prepped yet another bottle with formula. Sometimes, it felt like that was all she did.

She was juggling a whimpering Ariel with one arm while trying to mix the bottle with another when Eli approached. "I'll help." Instead of taking the bottle from her as she'd expected, he slid Ariel from her arms and walked toward the window, bouncing the baby as he went. "The two of us got to be best buds yesterday."

That was…interesting. Where he'd been so reluctant to even acknowledge Ariel just two days ago, he now seemed comfortable carting her around the room, murmuring something she couldn't understand. When the bottle was ready, Eli took it from her and continued to walk around, helping Ariel hold her dinner as he did.

Carly couldn't stop watching. What was happening? How did he go from baby terror to this so quickly? *Lord, what's going on? Are You…healing him? Somehow?* It was confusing and maybe a little scary to watch, and when Eli set the bottle on the table and continued to walk around the room with a cooing Ariel, she wasn't sure how to take it.

But she sure knew how to settle into a lawn chair and let someone else take the lead for a bit. It was nice.

As darkness descended outside, the cabin turned a deep blue, the stuff of dreams. A hushed peace settled over the space.

She was half dozing while Eli stood at the window, pointing to things outside and naming them for Ariel. He suddenly stepped back and drew the curtain. "Carly." His voice was low but sharp.

She as on her feet before she was totally awake. Something was wrong.

Eli met her halfway. "Take Ariel. Go into the bathroom. Shut the door and don't—"

A gunshot cracked through the trees as the front window shattered.

FOURTEEN

The bathroom door had barely clicked behind Carly when another shot blasted through the top windowpane. The bullet buried itself in the log wall. Whoever was shooting, it seemed they were aiming high in an attempt to scare, not to kill.

Death wasn't the threat, though. They would probably bust in any moment to take Ariel away.

As Eli drew his weapon, he said a silent prayer of thanks that he'd moved away from the window with Ariel when he had. It seemed whoever had opened fire had carefully chosen his aim and his moment. The movement at the edge of the clearing, the flash of dying daylight on what might have been glasses or a scope, had provided just enough time to move everyone to relative safety.

Ariel's gasping, screaming cries filled the cabin, loud even behind the closed door. She had to be terrified, as did Carly. He had to get them out of here to safety.

Could he sneak them out the back door, or was someone there waiting? There had been two people in the parking lot the day before, one smacking him around and another driving the getaway car. What if they were both here now?

Worse, what if this was his fault? What if they had followed him from Oak City? He'd been careful about not picking up a tail, but could they have tagged his vehicle? Could they be tracking him remotely?

Beside him, Wrangler stood at the ready, quivering from the desire to spring into action as he waited for a command. There was no way Eli would send his partner out blindly though. He needed to know what they were getting into. The thought of Wrangler getting shot in the line of duty was one of his worst fears and more than he wanted to think about right now.

Three shots came from outside, but they didn't hit the cabin.

A ping and a hiss made him wince.

They'd shot out his SUV's tires.

Their best avenue of escape was gone.

To have any hope of safety, they would have to flee on foot. Where would they go? Darkness was nearly complete. The closest town was a forty-five-minute drive away. The closest person to them was…

Isaac. If they could get to Isaac's cabin, they might have a chance, but they'd have to move quickly. He could fire two shots out the window, directed upward to send the gunman into hiding and then—

A massive crash, and the front door flew open. A man rushed in wearing jeans, a long-sleeved black tee, a dark baseball cap and a bandanna tied around his face. He cleared the room like a professional. He immediately spotted Eli and raised his pistol. "Put it down, man. I'm just here for the kid, not to hurt anybody."

Eli took aim as well. "Federal agent, *man.* The last thing you want to do is mess with me. You're not getting her." He didn't want to shoot anyone, but he had another option shaking with anticipation beside him. "Wrangler. *Stellen. Stellen.*"

His partner leaped, clearing the space to the door in one

bound. He latched onto the man's arm, snarling as though he could rip the guy in two. Had he not been trained well, he just might have.

The man cried out, flailing, but he managed to aim his pistol at Wrangler. "I'll kill him. Call him off." He ground out the words through teeth gritted with pain.

That was the last thing he wanted to do, but they were stuck. No vehicle. No help. If one of them were to be wounded… "Wrangler. *Terug. Terug.*"

Immediately, his partner released and returned to his side, watching him.

Holding his arm to his stomach, the man backed out the door, obviously believing he was temporarily defeated.

Interesting. He could have shot Wrangler, but he hadn't. What had made him back down when he had the advantage?

That was a puzzle for later. He'd be back, probably as soon as he made his way to a vehicle and got reinforcements.

There wasn't much time. Racing to the bathroom door, Eli threw it open to find Carly huddled in the corner. "Grab a bag for Ariel. You have thirty seconds." He took Ariel from her, helped her to her feet, and ushered her into the main room.

Carly moved quickly. Though she'd kept her backpack ready for a moment like this one, she still shoved baby formula, food, and diapers into the bag until it was about to burst. She took Ariel and watched him for instructions, no questions asked.

He wasn't about to give her any verbal indication of their destination. That man could be right outside, listening. Instead, he drew his weapon, called to Wrangler, then went to the back door and stepped outside. Once he was relatively certain the area was clear, he waved Carly forward.

It would be a treacherous trip, particularly in the dark, but there was nowhere else to go.

If they wanted to survive, they'd have to walk away from civilization and deeper into danger.

It felt like they'd been feeling their way through the darkness for hours.

Carly snuggled Ariel closer in her carrier. Thankfully, the rocking motion of her footsteps had put the baby to sleep. If she'd continued her terrified screaming, it was possible either Carly's eardrums would have burst or the cries would have been a homing beacon to whoever had shot up the cabin.

Eli had fallen horribly silent. He hadn't spoken a word since they'd left. After firing off a text when they'd been on the trail for about fifteen minutes, he'd shut off his phone then simply walked a couple steps ahead of her, surveying the trees constantly, his weapon at the ready.

Wrangler trailed them, acting as their rear guard.

Carly was the middle of the train. She prayed continuously, her mind whirling, her emotions too spent to feel fear or discomfort. There was only darkness and trees and one foot in front of the other. She kept one hand protectively over Ariel's exposed head as branches and limbs clawed at her arms and hair. They were led by starlight and shadow, nothing else.

Each step she took, she placed her foot carefully, the image of that horrible rattler slithering through her mind. She could step on one without realizing it, could have her life ended right here, could—

No. If she kept up that line of thinking, she would root to the spot. The biggest threat wasn't from the snakes in her mind…it was from the men who could be right behind them.

Eli had better know where he was heading, because she had no idea. Her throat was dry and raw, and she'd give her entire savings account, small as it was, for water. She should have grabbed some. Clearly, if left to her own devices, she'd probably die out here, deep in the middle of literal nowhere.

The sound of water broke through her thoughts, and she traced it to her left, where a creek widened, starlight glowing on the water. She looked behind her and in front of her, following the creek bed. It had been such a small trickle that she hadn't even realized Eli was following a stream until it began to broaden. So he *did* know where he was going.

He stopped and turned toward her, holstering his pistol. "We're going to Isaac's." He kept his voice low, as though he was afraid there were ears everywhere. "I haven't heard a tail, so we may be safe, but I'm not risking it. Another twenty minutes or so and we'll reach a lake. We'll have to cross by canoe. You up for it?"

"Do I have a choice?" She tried to push some levity into her voice, but she wasn't certain she had.

He chuckled. "Not unless you want to walk the long way around, and that's hours and miles longer."

"Canoe it is."

He moved to start walking again, then turned back and laid a hand on her fingers over Ariel's head. "I'm not going to let anything happen to either of you." His voice was steely. He turned away abruptly and moved forward without waiting to see if she fell in behind him.

She had too much time to think as they plodded on. Doubts and fears assailed her, but she kept them inside, where they bubbled like a shaken soda bottle.

Without warning, the trees opened up and the sky became visible, bright with stars like she'd never seen before. In front of them, a large lake reflected the sky. Carly's feet stuttered to a stop and, for an instant, she forgot everything but the deep blue sight in front of her. Out here, away from artificial light, the stars were incredible. There were so many of them.

They shone so bright and seemed to hang so low that she felt like she should be able to pull one down and hand it to Ariel.

The lake was so calm that it was a mirror, making it seem as though the entire galaxy had fallen to earth. The glory of it, the beauty of it, froze her feet in place. At any other time, she'd stand here and take it in for hours.

If God cared enough to create something so incredible, so beautiful, something that only a handful of people would ever lay eyes on, then surely he cared enough to watch over them, right?

Even Eli seemed mesmerized by the sight. "I've never been here at night before." The confession seemed to fall out without him realizing it. He stood and stared for a moment before he shook his head, squared his shoulders, and stepped back to stand beside her. "This is the most dangerous part of the trip." He kept his voice low. "Out there, we have nowhere to hide. Once we're in that canoe, our shadow on the water will be visible for miles. Are you sure you're ready for this?"

"I'm sure." She'd do anything for Ariel. If that meant making herself a sitting duck, then so be it.

She followed Eli to a long, narrow shed and watched as he disappeared inside. He dragged out a slim two-seater canoe. There was barely room for them, Wrangler and her bag.

She held Ariel a little closer. If they capsized…

Maybe this was a horribly bad idea. She froze, her hands splayed along Ariel's back in the carrier, a thousand what-ifs paralyzing her. She couldn't do this. She couldn't take another step.

When Eli handed her a life jacket, she stared at it. Could she do this?

She had to. To protect Ariel, there was no other choice.

As quickly as she could, she expanded the straps, then

fastened the life jacket around her and the still-sleeping baby, who was liable to burn up under so many layers if they didn't reach their destination soon.

The combination of warm baby, carrier, and life jacket was nearly too much heat for Carly as it was.

After sliding the canoe in the water, Eli returned. He eyed her in the starlight, seeming to sense her struggle. "It's half an hour on calm water, and the canoe is small enough that I can paddle alone. You take the front and worry about Ariel. I've got the rest." He dipped his head to look her in the eye. "Trust me."

She looked toward the water. Did she trust him?

Clearly she did. But ultimately…

She took a deep breath and tilted her chin to look skyward. Ultimately, despite everything in her life, she knew she wasn't in charge. Neither was Eli. Whatever happened next, for better or for worse, it was in bigger hands than either of theirs.

She'd asked Wendy once how she could stand to be married to a cop, one who might not come back someday.

Wendy's answer had been so certain. *Because in the end, God's in charge and already knows what's going to happen. If it's Mike's time, it's his time, whether he's on the street or asleep in his own bed.*

Carly took a deep breath. Violence had touched their lives so many times, and death had chased them all the way to the end. But she had no doubt that Wendy was right. God was ultimately still in charge, whether they were on that lake or safely tucked away in her house.

Although she'd much rather be in her house.

"Carly?" Eli was waiting for her to make the call.

"Let's go." Stepping around him before she could lose her nerve, she made her way to the boat and climbed in, taking the front seat as Wrangler jumped in behind her. The boat rocked and Ariel stirred, but then she settled down and drifted back to sleep.

Once again, Carly thanked God for a child who could apparently sleep through anything. Although, as Eli shoved off from shore, it was likely that being rocked to sleep was the best thing for Ariel.

It wasn't the best thing for her, though. The motion of the canoe as Eli paddled slowly and silently wasn't helping her exhaustion or the sick feeling in her stomach. She looked over her shoulder. "Do you think it's safe to talk?"

"Sound carries over water, but if we keep it low, then I don't think it will make us any more visible than we already are."

Something was digging at her, bothering her. "Why are they trying to take Ariel by force? They can't access any accounts or safe deposit boxes by just holding her up and announcing they have her. It takes legal paperwork, and they're doing their best to get that through the courts. Why would they try to wrench her away? It doesn't make sense."

There were several moments when the only sound was of the paddle digging in and the canoe sliding through the water. "I've been wondering that myself. Ultimately, I have no idea."

It felt like something else was happening, something she couldn't quite put her finger on. She stared into the darkness, the half an hour Eli had promised stretching into what felt like days.

Behind her, he was silent, all his energy going into paddling them across the lake.

When they finally reached the shore, it was well into the darkest part of the night, and Carly was ready to collapse on dry ground.

Eli beached the craft then helped her out, dropping her hand as quickly as he'd grabbed it. He hefted the backpack and called to Wrangler, who bounded to his side. "Less than a mile now, and we'll be at Isaac's. Let me go first. He's wary of visitors."

She followed him wordlessly. Something had happened in the cabin, something that had stolen his words and chilled the warmth he'd been showing her. Was it because she'd dared to kiss him? Or was it the danger that hunted them? Was he once again reminded of his wife and daughter?

Even if he did open up to her, would she ever be enough for him, or would he always be tied to his memories, with her taking second place?

She'd never been enough for anyone, not even her parents. They'd chosen drugs and themselves over her.

She'd certainly never felt like enough in any foster home she'd ever been placed in, and even the system had given up on her when she'd turned eighteen.

Only Mike and Wendy had viewed her as enough, but they'd had each other. She'd been added baggage.

Her whole life, she'd been a perpetual third wheel.

She trudged along until a cabin came into view, a dark shadow in the forest. Even the sight of it couldn't lift her weary heart or exhausted spirits.

From her worn-out mind, a new thought emerged.

What about Ariel? Would she ever be enough for her?

And would she be able to protect this tiny life from men determined to steal her?

FIFTEEN

"Thanks for letting us crash your party." Eli looked over at Isaac, who was busy casting his fishing line into the lake, having promised fresh fish for breakfast if they were biting.

Isaac sniffed, clearly not entirely thrilled with the intrusion to his solitary lifestyle, though he'd never verbalize it.

The night had been too short after they'd reached the cabin, Eli had convinced Isaac not to shoot, and they'd bedded down for the night. While Isaac's homestead was more remote that the hunting cabin, it was more spacious and included a rigged-up plumbing system that had allowed Carly to take a shower in water that had warmed in a tank on the roof. She'd expressed her gratitude multiple times before she'd climbed into a handmade twin bed in Isaac's bedroom. The older man had finally given her a genuine smile before the men bunked on cots in the main living area.

They'd risen early to fish for their breakfast. Eli would have been happy with eggs from the chickens scratching in a pen in the yard, but it seemed Isaac needed to be outside in the morning air.

If he was being honest, so did Eli.

"Been hard on you, has it?" Isaac cast his line again, as casually as if this conversation was a chat over coffee about the baseball scores. He was a man of few words but deep insight.

Isaac had no idea. This push-pull thing with Carly… The way he was tugged toward until his guilt and fears shoved him backward was exhausting. Add to it the search for Mia and the constant threat of attack and he was coasting on whatever level was below fumes.

He'd dreamed about Hailey in his fitful sleep last night, and it'd been the same dream as always. She smiled at him, then turned and walked away, disappearing as he woke up.

Every time.

He could never catch up to her.

Isaac reeled in his empty line and tried again. "I can see by your silence that I'm right."

"I lost everything. It was my fault. I'm not sure how to come back from that." The honesty spilled out without his permission. The confession seemed to hang like the morning mist over the lake, almost visible between them.

"I was thirty-two." Isaac's tone was matter-of-fact, just like earlier, like there was nothing more on the line than a Tuesday-night baseball game.

He didn't have to say any more. The pain beneath the words spoke as clearly to Eli as if Isaac had spilled his entire story. Still, he wanted to know. "What happened?"

"Brain tumor." Tipping back his ball cap, Isaac scratched his forehead then resettled his hat. "From the time we found out about it until the time she was gone was nine days."

Something tugged on Eli's line, but he ignored it. In all the years he'd come out to the cabin with his grandfather, he'd never known Isaac's story. The older man had always simply been his grandfather's friend, the slightly strange guy who lived in the middle of nowhere all alone.

Isaac's isolation made sense now, in some ways. In the days and weeks immediately after Hailey and Ivy died, Eli had wanted to hide from the world as well. A few nights, the bed had felt so big that he'd slept in the closet. It wasn't something he talked about, but it had happened. His world had shrunk, and he'd needed his space to shrink, too, or else he might have disappeared into some dark void he couldn't even fathom the size of.

Bird songs and the slow whirr and pause of Isaac's reel as he tempted the fish below the surface with the lure filled the space. The moment was for being still and remembering.

Hailey had been the love of his life. He'd fallen for her the moment she walked into his US history class in high school, and he'd never looked back. They'd planned and dreamed and cried together. They'd celebrated Ivy's impending arrival together. They'd endured arguments and disagreements and even a breakup right before they got married, but he'd always known he loved her. How to live without her had escaped him for too long, especially when every moment was dogged with guilt. Maybe if he'd been driving…

How could his heart dare to light up for another woman when he'd been blessed with Hailey? How dare he move forward when every dream had died with the ending of three lives violently snatched from this world by a bullet meant for him?

And yet, he lived.

What was it Carly had said? He was still here. His book was still being written. That beautiful, amazing chapter had ended. Was it time for a new one to begin? How would Hailey feel if he loved someone else? How would she feel if he *already* loved someone else?

It couldn't be the same.

His line went slack, but he barely noticed it.

It couldn't be the same. Maybe that was the point. Carly wasn't Hailey. Ariel wasn't Ivy. They were their own people with their own personalities.

He'd been drawn to Hailey's loud humor and gentle wisdom and live-life-to-the-fullest attitude. He was drawn to Carly's independence and fire, her sacrificial love and her bravery. Could he celebrate what he'd once had while glorying in a whole new life? Was that even possible? Could he—

"Even your grandfather didn't know this." Isaac broke through his thoughts. "Patricia was pregnant when she died. We found out because they tested her before they weighed treatment options. I literally found and lost a whole lifetime in nine days."

There was nothing to say to such pain, but there was a shared understanding in the words. While Eli hadn't realized that Isaac knew what he'd gone through, it was clear the older man knew his grief.

Eli reeled in the line, not at all surprised that the fish he'd felt earlier had slipped away. "How did you handle it?" Maybe he had some insight on how to move forward, how to continue living in the wake of tragedy, how to love someone new without feeling guilty for it.

"Handle it?" Isaac barked a laugh then swept his hand in an arc that encompassed the lake and maybe even the entire valley. "I came here. The world can't touch me here. I lost everything I loved. What else was there? What good was I as a man if I couldn't save my wife and my kid? Might as well pack it in. So I did. I made my own way right here where nobody could take anything away from me again. It's all in my control."

The words smacked like a slap. The only thing Eli had known on some nights was that he wasn't alone. It had been in those darkest hours that he'd cried out more to God. As he'd grieved, he'd come to realize he wasn't alone in that closet or in his room or anywhere else. While it had felt like a screaming anguish in the moment, he could look back and see all the ways God had shown up for him, in cards and letters and visits and even food left on his porch with no expectation of conversation. God had been in the nights he'd been able to finally sleep and in the days when he'd packed up Ivy's nursery and stored it away in his barn after the move. God had been in the fact that he hadn't come unglued and fallen completely apart, even when the pain felt so sharp that it might just rip him to shreds.

No, he'd never been alone, yet Isaac had chosen to go it alone.

That kind of emptiness felt heavy and sad.

With his grandfather around, there had always been a buffer between Eli and Isaac. The older man had seemed mysterious and cool, a real wilderness survivor. Only in the past couple of days had it become clear that Isaac wasn't a survivor. He was a dead man walking. He was closed off and alone, maybe even bitter and unwilling to open up to others. He wasn't happy. He hadn't found joy in the wilds. He'd found a pseudo-peace that came from shutting himself away from the world and pretending that meant everything was perfect.

Eli held the fishing pole but didn't cast. Instead, he studied the unruffled surface of the water. Was that what he wanted? To be closed off, shut away, feeling no new pain because he refused to feel no new joy? "Isaac, are you happy?"

Isaac stared across the lake, where the just-risen sun scattered sparkles across the clear water. "In a manner of speaking."

But not really.

"Some days it still hurts." It was a confession Eli had never made to anyone else, but it felt right in the moment.

"I imagine it always will. If it didn't, what you felt for your wife and your kid wouldn't have been love. You don't hand over chunks of your heart and expect your heart to ever be the same." Isaac cranked the reel slowly, keeping his eye on the line. "It seems like you're feeling some conflict, so I'm going to ask you one question."

Was he ready to answer?

When the line was fully in, Isaac propped the butt of his fishing pole on the ground and looked directly at Eli. "When you're with Carly… When you hold that baby… Do you see Carly and that baby? Or do you see your wife and your baby?" He lifted the fishing pole and walked closer, heading for the trail. When he reached Eli, he stopped and eyed him. "Me? No matter what woman I talked to or what kid I saw, I could never really see them. I only saw Patricia and who my kid might have been." He shouldered past. "And that's why I'm out here."

Eli turned and watched him walk up the trail. *Carly isn't Hailey. Ariel isn't Ivy.* His earlier thoughts circled back and brought a thrill of confirmation. When he was with them, he saw them, not some layered-over version of his past life.

He saw the here and now.

He saw the future.

Hailey had been the type to grab life and hold it close, to thrill in joy and to create experiences that made Eli feel alive. If she could talk to him now, would she want him to hide away in a wilderness of his own making? Or would she want him to embrace the life that God had set in front of him, something new and different and maybe even a little bit terrifying?

He knew the answer. The best way to love and honor her memory and Ivy's was to live in the joy she'd always poured out on others. The best way to love and honor them was to choose life.

But if he loved again, he could lose again. Was he ready to take that risk?

* * *

Carly rocked Ariel in the morning sunlight that flooded Isaac's front porch. Wrangler lay at her feet, basking in the newly risen sunlight. The handmade rocker creaked in a way that offered comfort, even if nothing in her world was safe.

Even if nothing in her world made sense.

Eli had powered down his phone as soon as they'd put some distance between them and his grandfather's cabin, probably out of an abundance of caution to prevent being tracked, but maybe she could ask to borrow it. She'd been doing a lot of thinking, and she might be able to get some legal answers from Julia Crosby.

Her contact info was in Carly's phone, which she'd left behind to avoid being tracked, but she didn't know it by heart. It shouldn't be hard to find with a quick search, since the assistant DA's office number was public information. As an older friend since the days they'd been in foster care, she'd offered to help Carly multiple times since Wendy had passed, and had even offered to babysit Ariel if Carly needed time to rest.

Carly looked down at the baby, who was seated in her lap and facing out to the world. Ariel alternated between playing with her own fingers and studying the dust that glittered in the sunlight spilling over them through the trees. Maybe she should take Julia up on that offer for a few days until they figured out what was going on. Surely an assistant DA could offer the kind of protection that Carly and Eli couldn't, or maybe Julia could get them to a safe house that was truly safe.

She twisted her lips. The only hesitation she had there was that Julia worked closely with the Oak City PD. The woman had always been friendly to Wendy and even to Carly. She'd been an advocate for justice in the wake of

Mike's murder, seeking answers and pushing the department to locate suspects.

Still, she'd been Mike's friend more than Wendy's and she had ties to the OCPD, so could she be trusted?

If there was even the off chance that she was involved in nefarious dealings, Carly was scared to reach out. In truth, she was scared of everyone right now…except Eli.

It was shocking that she trusted Eli. She bounced Ariel on her knee and watched the path the men had walked down to the lake. Her upbringing hadn't been stable or easy, and her time on the streets had taught her that more people were out to scam you than to help you…or so she'd believed. She'd always trusted Wendy and Mike, but now it seemed that Mike could have violated not only Wendy's trust but the entire community's as well. It was so hard to believe that could be true.

But Eli… She rocked slowly as Ariel babbled away. Eli she trusted.

The trees rustled and Isaac appeared through the leaves, carrying a bucket and a fishing pole. He barely acknowledged her as he walked around the corner of the cabin and disappeared.

Her heart rate skipped once when Eli stepped into the clearing, and Wrangler jumped up to join him. Eli carried only a fishing pole, and he glanced at her with a quick, almost hesitant smile as he followed Isaac around the cabin. No wave. No *good morning*. Just that reserved smile.

Her heart sank. She hadn't seen *that* smile since the first time she'd passed him while jogging on the road nearly a year ago. It was a smile reserved for strangers or mild acquaintances, not one given to a woman who might have captured a piece of his heart the way she'd thought. He'd certainly captured a piece of hers.

She gathered Ariel close and stood. Walking to the top of the wooden porch steps, she scanned the ground for snakes then stepped into the small pine-straw-covered yard. Eli shouldn't be a consideration right now. Her priorities were with Ariel and with keeping her safe. They couldn't hide out in the forest forever. Maybe—

"Isaac's got fish on and some eggs from his chickens." The porch behind her creaked as if to emphasize Eli's announcement. "It's not the kind of breakfast you get in town but, trust me, it's standard out here and it's delicious."

When she turned, he was watching her with Wrangler at his side. Something in his expression was guarded, like he had thoughts he wasn't ready to express. Not that he owed her access to his inner musings, but it did seem he'd shared increasingly more as the months had passed.

She'd love to know what he was thinking now.

But again, there were bigger concerns. She shifted Ariel to her other hip. "I need to go back."

Eli's head jerked slightly, as though she'd landed a blow, then his expression tightened. "It's too dangerous."

"So is staying there." She waved her free hand in the direction of the lake they'd crossed the night before. "They found us at your grandfather's cabin. How long before they find us here? Last night, I canoed across a dark lake with Ariel, praying the entire time we wouldn't capsize. I trekked through the dark woods terrified of crashing into a spiderweb or stepping on the cousin of that snake that nearly ended both of our lives earlier. I can't do this anymore."

The more she talked, the more she became acutely aware that her reserves were running dry. It was worse because of her whiplashing and increasing feelings for Eli. "I need a real place for Ariel to sleep and real food for me to eat and a real shower and—" Tears clogged her throat. She was strong, but roughing it the past few days had brought up too many memories she'd managed to bury, too many parallels to living wherever she could find a place to lay her head for the night, safe or not.

With a heavy exhale, Eli put one arm around her and pulled her to his side, resting his other hand on Ariel's back. He laid his chin on the top of Carly's head and was silent, once again letting her cry.

Wrangler leaned against her leg as though he knew she needed a little something more.

The storm didn't last long. She'd already spent so many tears that she felt like she was nearly dry. Swiping her free hand over her cheeks, she could feel the heat there. "I'll bet you think all I do is fall apart."

His arm around her tightened. "Who wouldn't in this situation? You've been through a lot. Most people would have run screaming into the mountains by now." His shoulders moved with each breath, and she could feel his heartbeat. "I'll tell you what." The words rumbled in his chest, low and comforting. "Let me get my feet under me and figure out how they tracked us to the cabin. I'll use Isaac's cell and avoid turning mine on, just in case it was compromised. Once I feel like we can safely do so, I'll get with my team and we'll move you into a safe house more suited to Ariel's needs until this is all sorted out."

The thought was both a relief and a jolt. Going to a safe house might mean that Eli would leave her in someone else's care.

She wasn't ready to *not* be with him. He was the only person she truly felt safe with.

At the same time, she had to consider Ariel, and she had to be aware of her own need for some sort of routine and sanity…and hot water.

"Breakfast!" Isaac's gruff call came from the back of the house.

Pulling his arm away, he gestured toward the corner of the cabin. "Think you can stomach fish and eggs for breakfast?"

"On a normal day, no." Even now, the thought was slightly off-putting. "But given that it's hot food? I'd eat that canoe if you grilled it." She needed some sort of levity, or she'd never survive.

They headed for the corner of the cabin, but Wrangler stayed where he was, staring toward the lake.

Eli stepped back toward him and looked in that direction while Carly waited for them. "What's up, partner? You mad I left you here when we went fishing?"

Interesting. She hadn't considered that Wrangler had been ordered to stay by her side but, come to think of it, he normally shadowed Eli. That meant that, even out here, Eli didn't trust that she was safe alone.

He gestured toward Carly and Ariel. "Wrangler, *hier.*"

For the first time in Carly's experience, Wrangler hesitated, but then he looked up at Eli and trotted around the corner of the cabin.

Eli eyed the lake, then walked with Carly and Ariel to the rear of the cabin, where a low, rough-hewn table was surrounded by wooden Adirondack chairs. A cast-iron skillet of fish and another of eggs sat over a nearby campfire, and metal plates were stacked on the table. An old percolator sat on the table with tin cups beside it.

The blended scent of coffee and fish and eggs was actually appetizing enough to make Carly's stomach rumble. Even Ariel wriggled, recognizing that certain scents meant there was food nearby.

Carly leaned over her charge. "Pretty sure you're not ready for fish or eggs yet. It's a bottle and baby food for you."

When she headed for the back door of the cabin to do something toward making that bottle, Isaac stepped out, carrying one that was already made.

Carly arched an eyebrow at the sight of the older man in his jeans and long-sleeved tee, awkwardly holding a baby bottle in one giant hand.

He pinked slightly. "What? I can read the back of a can." He passed her the bottle and kept walking, pulling the pans from the fire and settling them on the low table. "Eat before it's cold. Nothing is worse than cold eggs."

Exchanging a smile with Eli, who waved her into a seat, Carly settled into an Adirondack chair with Ariel and let the baby take the bottle.

Eli fixed her plate, and they all settled down in a comfortable silence, punctuated by birdsong and a slight breeze in the treetops. In any other situation, she'd have called the morning peaceful and perfect.

Except for Wrangler. The K-9 kept pacing, and Eli kept having to call him back from the side yard.

Carly didn't miss that Eli's brow creased with concern or that he kept a careful eye on the direction his partner was focused on. The edginess stole her peace, and Ariel picked up on it, fussing with her bottle and shoving it away.

Before she could ask what she was missing, Wrangler suddenly trotted to Eli's side and looked up as though he was waiting for a command.

Eli and Isaac stood at the same time, setting their plates aside.

"Carly, go inside and shut the door." Eli's voice was tense, and he reached for his gun.

"What's—" But a new sound silenced the birds and hummed louder than the breeze.

A boat engine on the lake, approaching quickly.

Her stomach twisted.

They'd been found once again.

SIXTEEN

As soon as Carly and Ariel disappeared into the cabin, Eli drew his pistol and looked over at Isaac, who had grabbed the rifle he kept nearby in case of wild animals.

Unless he missed his guess, the two of them were about to confront the wildest animals of all. He just prayed it wouldn't lead to a gunfight.

Commanding Wrangler to stay at his side, Eli walked around the cabin with Isaac close behind, keeping careful watch as he did. Though the two of them had never worked together before, they fell into a step that had them seamlessly moving as though they'd trained for this very moment. It likely had to do with both of them being trained law enforcement officers.

Two men appeared out of the trees, approaching warily but not confrontationally.

Oak City Police Officer Paul Cantor led the way, and a man wearing jeans and a button-down shirt followed close behind.

Eli had worked with the younger officer on a couple investigations and had always believed the officer to be aboveboard. The second man was vaguely familiar, but Eli couldn't quite place where he'd seen him before.

Motioning for Isaac to lower his rifle, Eli holstered his

pistol but kept his hand near it. With the possible corruption at Oak City PD and with the identity of the men who'd attacked both him and Carly still unknown, he was wary even of people he'd once trusted. "Cantor. What brings you out here? And who's this with you?"

Holding both hands in front of him as though he didn't want a confrontation, Cantor pressed his lips tightly in a grim line. "It's official business, and not necessarily business I'm pleased to be performing."

The hair on the back of Eli's neck went up. Was the officer telling the truth, or was he keeping them busy while other bad actors surrounded them?

He glanced down at Wrangler, who was focused on the men in front of them and not on the woods around them. His partner had likely heard the boat's engine long before they had, and that would account for his earlier antsy behavior. If anyone was creeping around in the woods, Wrangler would alert.

Eli turned his focus back to the men. "Official business for who? You don't have jurisdiction here. We're outside the city limits by a really good bit. And how did you know we'd be here? And, once again, you have yet to introduce your friend."

Cantor stopped at the edge of the clearing, his expression tight but not menacing. Either he was a very good actor, or he was on the up-and-up and wasn't thrilled with his reason for being here. Neither was a comforting thought.

Cantor nodded toward Isaac. "Isaac Gunderson used to be an Oak City cop, and plenty of us know where he lives. It didn't take much digging to figure out you'd either be at your grandfather's cabin or here."

"Have *you* been to my grandfather's cabin?" Eli's fingers ached to wrap around his pistol's grip just to remind himself he had a way to defend Carly and Ariel, but he didn't dare. He didn't want the hint of a threat to result in a shootout because someone got jumpy. "Someone came in with guns blazing last night."

The way Cantor's eyes blinked spoke to his surprise. He looked over his shoulder at the unidentified man as if asking a question, but the stranger's face remained blank. Cantor turned back to Eli. "I know nothing about that. Somebody shot at you? Why didn't you call it in? We'd have backed you up." The words and the facial expressions seemed sincere.

Did he dare trust the man?

No way was he letting his guard down. "Too much has happened for me to believe that at the moment." He sounded paranoid. It wouldn't surprise him if Cantor didn't call in some reinforcements to deal with him and what could be deemed as strange behavior. "I've recently found out there are some cops on the force taking substantial bribes, and they're after Mike Higgins's daughter as a way to access the money he stashed."

Cantor's eyes widened, and uncertainty skittered across his face. Once again, he looked at the man behind him. "Are you not telling me something?" His hand went to his side-arm as he watched the stranger.

The other man held up his hands in a gesture of surrender. "Officer, you were directed by the district attorney's office to lead me here. Everything is aboveboard. I'll get the paperwork from my pocket. You've already seen it, and you know it's valid." Slowly, he reached around behind him and pulled something from the back pocket of his jeans, then held it up and handed it to Cantor, who glanced at it then approached Eli.

Wrangler growled low in his throat but didn't twitch a muscle.

Cantor shook his head slightly as he held out the papers. "I don't know what you've gotten yourself into, Officer Blackwood, but I'm here on this order to take the child, Ariel Danielle Higgins, into state custody and deliver her to the Colorado Department of Human Services until the court case determining who has guardianship of her has been decided. The paperwork is from the assistant DA."

Eli didn't take the paper.

Something was off. Oak City PD had zero jurisdiction in the wilderness. That would fall to the county or even the state. The DA wouldn't have anything to do with a child custody case, and Cantor should know that.

He looked from the paper to the officer to the stranger. Suddenly, recognition clicked.

The photo that Eva had sent of the possibly crooked attorney behind the guardianship paperwork. Dominic Gunther.

He glanced to his right, where Isaac was watching him as intently as Wrangler was. He had no doubt the man would have his back if necessary.

"No." Eli shook his head and took a step closer to the two men. "That paperwork means nothing out here. If you want to take Ariel, you'll have to do it legally." This was all fishier than the breakfast they hadn't gotten a chance to eat.

Wrangler growled again, the sound menacing and low.

That was an alert, one that indicated he'd picked up on something that Eli hadn't. Someone was around who wasn't visible. "Who else is with you?"

"No one." Cantor looked surprised by the question.

Gunther did not. In fact, the man looked a little smug, like he thought he had the upper hand.

It was a trap. "Carly! Hide!"

Two more men stepped out of the woods with rifles aimed straight at him and at Isaac, and the jaws of the trap snapped shut.

Carly rushed into the bathroom. How many different bathrooms could she take cover in?

Ariel screamed and cried, struggling to get free as Carly held her close. She shoved the bathroom door shut, but there was no lock. Of course not. Why would a solitary man even need a door, let alone a lock?

She huddled in the corner of the tiny shower, the floor still wet, holding Ariel close as the baby's cries increased in pitch and intensity.

"It's okay. I've got you. It's okay." She whispered desperate comfort when she felt none herself, all while silently screaming incoherent prayers for God to make all the craziness stop.

From the front of the cabin, the murmur of voices raised and lowered, but there were thankfully no gunshots...yet.

What was happening? Who was here? Why was someone doing this to them?

Maybe it was Eli's team and not someone out to hurt them. She prayed it was so, that help had arrived and that they were safe.

Please, Lord. Hadn't they been through enough?

Her mind spun so fast that she couldn't pray any longer. The terror was too real. The longing for safety was too strong. She'd never before wanted the four walls of her own house around her so badly.

She saw no end in sight. Wherever she ran, these men would find her, would find Ariel. They were literally in the middle of nowhere, completely off the grid, yet the threat had arrived on their doorstep yet again.

It was too much.

If it wasn't for Ariel needing to be protected, she'd give up. Surrender. Put the madness to an end.

But Ariel needed her, so she'd dig deep and fight until her last breath to protect Wendy's daughter, who'd wrapped tiny little fingers around her heart.

But was there any real way out? Wasn't there anyone who could—

The back door creaked open and footsteps fell on the wide board floor.

Carly held her breath.

The boards creaked under the weight of a person, and footsteps inched closer to the door. Drawing her knees to her chest and curling her body around Ariel, she did her best to protect the little girl she loved more than she loved her own life.

There was no doubt this was a foe, not a friend. A friend would have called out to her.

It certainly wasn't Eli. Even above the pounding of her pulse in her ears, she could still discern his voice from the front of the cabin.

It had to be one of the men who'd come after them before.

She wanted to scream, to shout, to alert Eli that someone was inside, but the words stuck in her throat.

She wanted to burst through the bathroom door and run, but her muscles refused to comply.

It was just like that night in the culvert, when danger stalked her and she was helpless to defend herself.

She was frozen, drowning in a waking nightmare, as the footsteps came closer...closer...

Then stopped.

The door swung open.

The man who'd chased her to Eli's stood in the doorway,

a pistol leveled directly at her. He smirked when he saw the fear on her face. "Looks like I win. This time, you have nowhere to run."

SEVENTEEN

Eli calculated his odds. The underhanded lawyer, Dominic Gunther, was clearly a foe. The two men to his left and right were obviously not friendly. Officer Paul Cantor was a wild card.

Wrangler could handle one assailant. Isaac another. And he himself could take on one more.

That left the wild card. Was Cantor a pawn in whatever was happening? Or was he one of the cops who had a hand in the bribery cookie jar? Would he help Eli, or would he draw his weapon in opposition?

Dominic Gunther stepped in front of Officer Cantor, his swagger indicating he fully believed he was in charge. Clearly, he couldn't count. "Officer Blackwood, I'm here to take Ariel Higgins to a home where she'll be safe."

There was no mention of children's services this time. Gunther was up to something. "Whose home? She's with her guardian." He was stalling to think, but he also might get some answers.

Gunther hesitated, but he quickly recovered. "It doesn't matter. You need to bring her to me."

Resting his hand on his pistol, Eli took a step closer, keeping an eye on the men wielding rifles. "If this were legal, you wouldn't have brought your brute squad along." He spoke to

Gunther, but he kept his eyes over the man's shoulder on Officer Cantor, who was watching the two newcomers warily. *Come on, man, be a friend.*

"Eli." Carly's voice came from behind him.

He didn't take his eyes off the threat. "Carly, go back inside. Now." What was she thinking, showing her face in front of armed men? Didn't she realize—

"Eli, it's over. We don't have a way out. We have to…" Her voice cracked. "He'll hurt Ariel."

"I'd listen to her, Officer Blackwood." A new voice entered the conversation, a deep male voice tinged with derision and twisted amusement.

Isaac's growl almost matched Wrangler's. "Eli, you should look. I'll keep eyes on these guys."

Something was wrong. Very wrong. He could sense the tension thicken around him, could feel the panic surge in his gut. Glancing over his shoulder, he spotted Carly holding Ariel at the bottom of the front porch steps.

A man stood one step above her. He was older than Eli and had a muscular build. Although he'd shaved his head, aged and bulked up, Eli recognized him from the photo Eva had sent. It was Les Cassel, a former OCPD officer.

Cassel's jaw was set in determination. His eyes held a challenge that said he knew he'd won.

The man's appearance had barely registered before Eli saw the pistol pressed against the base of Carly's skull.

Panic iced over his mind and his body. He couldn't feel his heartbeat, couldn't feel anything. His brain seemed to exit his skull to float somewhere above him, as if he was watching everything happen from a distance.

He'd failed.

Again.

The woman he'd grown to trust and love was in danger. The child in her arms was in danger.

He couldn't protect them. Couldn't prevent this. There was no good way for this to end.

Time stopped.

He wanted to double over against the pain, to shout an apology to Carly, to—

"The past is the past." Eli's low mutter barely reached his ears, but it cut through the fog and sank into his core. "This is today."

Reality returned in a rush. Time picked up speed. He'd failed in the past, but that wasn't who he was. He could end this. He could protect Carly and Ariel. He could succeed. *Show me how, Lord.*

He couldn't do it alone.

Cassel spoke with a cockiness that might just be his downfall. "Officer, we'll be going now. I'll leave Carly on the other side of the lake after I know you haven't followed in an attempt to stop me from taking the kid." He leveled a threatening gaze on Eli. "Here's the thing you need to realize… I don't care a bit about the kid, not as much as the person who's giving me orders. That kid's a paycheck, sure, but she's not worth my life. So don't think I'll hesitate the way you would if the chips went down."

The threat was clear. He'd hurt Ariel to save himself. If she wasn't important to him, who was she important to? Who would pay someone to steal a child while simultaneously forging documents to get custody?

None of this made sense. What was happening, and why?

None of that mattered.

Only the next few seconds counted.

He forced his mind into logical thought. He deliberately made eye contact with Officer Cantor, who was watching him. The other man gave a slight nod, a glint of steel in his eyes.

He was on Eli's side. The fight was even.

But only if he could get that gun away from Carly's head.

He hoped Isaac could read his mind.

Eli nodded slowly, dragging his gaze from Carly to Isaac. "Today is today." He shifted his gaze to the man at their right, desperate for Isaac to understand.

Isaac blinked once. He understood.

If Eli was going to get through this, he couldn't be the one to deal with Cassel while he was holding a gun to Carly's head. He'd hesitate.

But Wrangler wouldn't.

Eli looked at Officer Cantor, shifting his gaze to Dominic Gunther. *Take him.* "Okay. You win." Slowly, he bent his knee as if to settle his gun on the ground.

The two armed men at the edge of the clearing stepped closer.

As Eli knelt, he used his elbow to nudge Wrangler toward Cassel.

It was now or never.

"Wrangler! *Stellen! Stellen!*"

At the command to attack, the clearing exploded with motion.

Carly screamed.

Isaac's rifle fired.

Eli took aim at the man on the left and pulled the trigger as the man turned his rifle toward Eli.

Officer Paul Cantor whirled on Dominic Gunther and drew his sidearm, aiming it at the man's heart. "I suggest you stay right there."

In the echo of gunfire, the only sounds were Wrangler's growl and a series of angry, pained, unintelligible curses.

Eli turned toward Carly. She stood pressed against the porch railing, holding Ariel close, her eyes wide as her entire body shook.

With a vicious jerk, Wrangler dragged Les Cassel off the steps and stood over him as he lay on the ground, fear replacing his earlier arrogance.

Isaac stepped around Eli and retrieved Cassel's fallen pistol. "I've got him."

Good, because Eli was pretty sure his adrenaline was crashing. "Wrangler. *Los. Kom hier.*"

The dog obediently let go and trotted to Eli's side, looking up in expectation. Gifting his partner with an ever-present treat from the pocket of his cargo pants, he stepped over to Carly as Isaac and Cantor worked on taking the others into custody.

He holstered his sidearm and didn't stop moving until she was in his arms, against his chest with Ariel between them. "I've got you. Both of you. You're safe." He hoped. Just because the attorney who had filed the paperwork was in custody, that didn't mean this was over.

Who knew how many people were after the money that only guardianship of Ariel could grant them access to? Did it matter to any of them that they wouldn't be able to access the cash anyway because it was likely going to be seized as a part of the bribery investigation?

And worse, who was paying that man to take Ariel?

"Eli?" Isaac's voice cut through his thoughts. "There's work to do."

It was Carly who understood the words first. Her shoulders rose with a deep breath, then she stepped out of his arms. "I'm fine. Wrap this up and then we'll talk."

She knew his heart and understood how much he wanted

to stay with her, but he needed to make sure all of this was wrapped up so that she and Ariel were safe.

With a long last look, he released her and turned toward Officer Cantor, who had handcuffed Dominic Gunther. "Get somebody in her quickly. Boat, helicopter, whatever, just get these guys out of here." He'd have to hitch a ride with them and give his statement, as would Carly. Isaac would likely refuse to leave and have to be debriefed out here at the cabin.

Cantor moved to help Isaac restrain Les Cassel. "Eli, I had no idea. I was called in by the assistant DA and told to assist with this, that it was a special assignment. Those guys are all cops, and I thought… I had no idea—"

"We can talk about it later." He gave the man a grateful nod. "But thank you for jumping in to help." He needed to get Carly and Ariel to safety. The rest could wait. "Have the county or the state send us two ways out. I want Carly and Ariel in a safe house until we know this is truly over." He expected her to argue, but she was silent.

Isaac stepped up. "I'll go with Carly and the kid."

Eli whipped toward him, more shocked than he had been by anything else that had happened in the past few minutes. "Are you sure?" Isaac voluntarily leaving his "fortress of solitude" for anything other than supplies was very out of character. "I'd appreciate it."

"Me, too." Carly's words were quiet. "I trust him."

He heard the relief in her voice.

He just wished he could feel it as well.

"I'm pretty sure we've rounded up everyone who was involved. Officer Cantor is still on scene, aiding there, and we'll get his statement as soon as he returns." Oak City Police Chief Roland Andrews stood at the front of the brief-ing room and addressed the handful of people sitting at the tables before him. It was a select group of Oak City detectives, a few Internal Affairs investigators, and Eli. The department was interested in keeping the bribery scheme on the down-low as much as possible until they could release an official statement.

As soon as Dominic Gunther had been brought into interrogation, he'd started talking, pointing fingers at anyone and everyone who had taken even one single bribe. It seemed that Mike Higgins had been the "treasurer" of a group of four current and former officers who had been taking bribes for years. The three surviving members who were still on the police force had gathered at Isaac's cabin to take Ariel.

Les Cassel had been a harder nut to crack, offering up a few scarce details that they'd already suspected.

Although Mike was the newest member of the group, he'd been the most tech savvy and had suggested the cryptocurrency wallet. While the group had kept some of the cash, Mike had squirreled away the money to hide the build of it.

But then Ariel had been born. Something had changed after the birth of his daughter, and his guilty conscience had led him to consider confessing the whole thing. The others had decided he was a liability.

Les Cassel had pulled the trigger to silence Mike but, in their panic, the group hadn't considered how to access the crypto key in the safe deposit box. Their initial plan had been to wait a couple months and then to approach Wendy with an offer to split the money, but she'd died before they could put that plan into action. They claimed to have had no part in her death.

Cassel had confessed to devising the scheme to get custody of Ariel. The group had hired Dominic Gunther to falsify documents and bring the case forward, but they'd rapidly realized they didn't need to wait for the case to go to trial if

Gunther could forge documents that said Ariel was already theirs. He'd agreed to take a substantial amount of money in return for creating a paper trail that said Les Cassel was Ariel's guardian.

None of that explained why they'd tried to kidnap the baby. All they'd need to access the box was the paperwork. Why were they so desperate to get their hands on Ariel?

Cassel refused to comment on what he'd planned to do with Ariel once he had her, and Gunther swore he didn't know, that he'd merely been the forger.

Cassel was hiding something, and he hadn't been working alone. Someone else wanted Ariel. Eli's gut said so. A memory tickled the back of his mind, but he couldn't grab onto it and wrestle it into the light. There was an answer, but what was it?

Oak City PD was working with the Colorado Bureau of Investigation to ensure that everything was cleaned up and handled carefully. Hopefully, they'd find answers quickly.

As the meeting broke up, Eli spoke to a few of the officers and offered updates on the task force's investigation and the search for Mia. The officers at OCPD were keeping their eyes and ears open as well.

All he wanted was to get to the safe house where Carly and Ariel were waiting with Isaac. He needed to know they were both okay, and he had things he wanted to discuss.

As he walked to his SUV, where Wrangler waited in his special compartment, his cell phone rang.

Emmett.

Hopefully, the head of the task force had good news. It seemed like every turn they took lately led to one more dead end. He held the phone to his ear. "Did we find Mia?" Perhaps following his arrest at the clinic, Benny had cracked and said something that could lead to her.

"Hello to you, too." Emmett's voice crackled with sarcasm, but then he got down to business. "And I wish I could say we had, but no. There's a briefing in one hour at HQ if you can be there."

His heart sank. He wanted to get to Carly, but he couldn't bail on a case that was urgent.

He felt the sting of the past rearing up, the guilt of not being there when Hailey had needed him, but he prayed it down. *Today is today.* It was his new refrain.

Emmett was still talking. "How's your wrap-up going? Lizzie has kept me updated on your return to civilization."

Eli passed on the intel he'd just learned in the briefing and shared his confusion over the attempts to kidnap Ariel. "I can't make that make sense."

"You're right. If they simply wanted access to the money, forging docs would be the easiest way. If they weren't certain that was going to work, then taking Carly and Ariel and forcing Carly to access the box would have been the second easiest way. But *only* wanting Ariel? Just carrying a baby around and holding her out like some sort of proof of life isn't going to get them anywhere without legal docs."

"Exactly."

Emmett was silent for a moment. "Whose name was on the forged custody paperwork?"

"Les Cassel's." Eli scanned the parking lot, feeling antsy. Carly was at the safe house with Isaac, and he was ready to see her, to have a talk about their future, however slowly it might need to move. He still had a few things to work through, but he had no doubt he wanted to work through them with her.

"Anyone else?" Emmett's voice brought him back into the conversation.

"No. Cassel was the one claiming custody, and Dominic

Gunther was his attorney. They brought in an OCPD officer, Paul Cantor, and had him believe that the DA's office—" *Hang on a sec.* That was it. That was the thing that didn't fit. "Emmett, why would the DA be involved in a custody case?"

"He wouldn't. Is that what your guys said?"

"I'd say they were lying, but Officer Paul Cantor said he was called in by the DA's office for a special assignment. That's a little suspect, but I'd assume he's smart enough to have to have been actually called in by someone there. He wouldn't just take Gunther's word for it."

"So you think someone at the DA's office wants Ariel? Why? If it was for the money, it still doesn't answer your question about why they'd physically want a baby."

"Hang on." Eli scrolled through his phone, praying he'd saved Cantor's contact info somewhere. He had. Hopefully he was headed back from the cabin and was close enough to a tower that a text would go through.

Who did you talk to at the DA's office?

He stared at the phone waiting…waiting…
Three dots.

The assistant DA. Julia Crosby.

EIGHTEEN

Carly stood over the pack-and-play, which had been wedged into a corner of the small upstairs bedroom in a cramped town house that Oak City PD used as a safe house. She watched Ariel sleep, the little one's breathing loud in the quiet room.

She sank to the edge of the double bed and stared at the doorway. It had been several hours since she'd been dropped off here with Isaac and with a police officer sitting at the end of the driveway. She'd hoped that Eli would come by, but she was starting to lose hope.

From downstairs, she could hear Isaac moving around. He'd been antsy since they'd arrived, probably missing his cabin and ready to head back. She'd told him that he could leave, but he'd developed a protectiveness over them, so she'd come upstairs to settle Ariel down for a nap and to let Isaac be alone.

Being alone herself had only let her thoughts drift to Eli. Maybe everything that had passed between them had been in her imagination. When it was safe for her to return home, would everything go back to what it had been? Friendship and nothing more?

She prayed not. Out at the cabin, she'd allowed herself to

admit that she'd grown to love Eli Blackwood over the past few months. He was becoming home to her, the kind of—

A crash sounded downstairs, and Carly jumped to her feet, headed for the door.

"Carly!" Isaac's shout was frantic. "Get—"

Another thump, then silence.

Carly's heart hammered. What was happening? She froze in the doorway, panic robbing her of thoughts and of strength. There was nowhere to hide, no way to get Ariel out of the house without going down the stairs and straight toward whatever had happened.

She whirled, turning toward the window. There was a police officer right outside, wasn't there? Maybe if she yelled—

She was two steps across the room when a rustle came from the doorway. "Carly?" A female voice spoke gently behind her. "It's okay. It's me. Julia Crosby."

Julia? What was she doing here? Was this truly some crazy nightmare? Had stress wrecked her mind?

She turned slowly, certain she was imagining everything, but it was indeed Julia standing in the doorway. Tall and lithe, Julia looked younger than her fortyish years, dressed in black dress pants and a formfitting red button-down. Her dark hair was pulled back in a high ponytail. As usual, she looked as though she'd stepped off a runway.

"Julia? What's happening? Where's Isaac?" Behind the confusion, there was a swirl of relief. Julia had been a friend first to Mike and then to Wendy, had doted on Ariel, and had been around the house nearly as much as Carly had in the wake of Mike's death. She loved the little family almost as her own, so if she was here then…then everything must be okay.

Carly nearly sagged in relief. She rested her palm against the cool wall to keep from sinking to the floor.

"It's over." Julia stepped into the room, her eyes sweeping the space until she saw Ariel. "It's time to take this little girl home."

Home. A real nursery. Her own clothes. Her safe place.

Weariness robbed her of her strength. It was over. They were going to be okay.

Julia stepped closer to the pack-and-play, her focus on the sleeping baby. "I'll take Ariel now."

What did that mean? Carly straightened. Alarm bells rang. Something in Julia's tone was off. The words that should have sounded comforting sounded vaguely threatening.

Moving quickly, she stepped around the foot of the bed and stood between the pack-and-play and Julia. She repeated her earlier question with more emphasis. "What's going on?"

Tilting her head so that her ponytail swung to the side, Julia pulled her gaze from Ariel and pinned Carly as though she was a bug on display. "I'm here to take Ariel home with me. She's my daughter, and it's time you stopped denying it and handed her over."

The words didn't compute. They made zero sense. "Ariel's not yours." The confusion was thick in her skull, preventing her from processing. "Where's Isaac?" She needed help, someone to stop whatever this was, to take Julia away and prevent her from succeeding in—

"She's mine." Julia took one step closer.

What was Julia talking about? Carly had been there on the night Ariel was born. She was definitely Wendy's daughter. "I think you're confused, Julia." Where was Isaac? Where was the police officer? "Isaac! Get help!"

Julia shook her head. "Isaac can't go get help. And even if he could, I sent the cop on an errand. He didn't think he could refuse the assistant district attorney."

Carly couldn't take much more. Her head was pounding

and her skin sheened with sweat. What had Julia done to Isaac? What was she going to do to Ariel? To her? Carly's mind screamed prayers.

She forced herself to think. She'd been in tighter spots than this, but never with a child to protect. She could do this. She had to do this. She was stronger than Julia thought she was. The trick was to keep the other woman talking while she planned. "How is Ariel yours?" Squaring her shoulders, trying to make herself look larger, Carly took one step toward Julia.

Julia held her ground. "I always wanted a baby." Julia's gaze shifted lovingly to Ariel, sleeping soundly and unaware of the danger. "Bruce couldn't have children. I knew Mike from when you were all younger. Did you know I helped him get his job on the police department?"

When Carly didn't respond, Julia kept talking, anger darkening her features. "I knew about the bribes, the money, what it could do to Mike's career, so I leveraged it. Told him if he could help me have a child, I could make things go away."

Carly swallowed nausea. She couldn't possibly be hearing this. Surely Mike wouldn't—

"He said he'd consider it." Julia's face clouded and she addressed the pack-and-play as though she'd forgotten Carly was in the room. "Two days later, Mike was killed, and I lost that leverage, that chance." She whirled on Carly, rage in her eyes. "I should have Mike's child. Wendy didn't understand that. I tried to tell her. She couldn't provide for the baby like I could. I had to make it happen, but I didn't count on you." She advanced one step. "You got in my way."

The words came out in a roar. Julia's hand struck out and grabbed Carly's hair, jerking downward.

Ariel cried out at the noise.

Stars dotted her vision from the violent twist in her neck,

and she cried out in pain. She reached up, trying to claw at Julia's hands, her fingernails digging into flesh.

Julia twisted harder, dragging her toward the floor.

There was no telling what would happen if she got her down. Carly fought, struggled, dug her nails in harder. This was for Ariel. This was for—

"Federal agent! Let her go and lace your hands behind your head!"

The world froze at the shout. Julia stopped moving. Carly breathed heavily, scared she was imagining the sound of Eli's voice.

"Do it now, Julia." Eli's voice was sharp and commanding.

Julia released Carly so quickly that she nearly dropped to the floor, but she braced one hand on the bed and managed to stand.

Eli stood in the doorway, his weapon drawn. A police officer was behind him, and Isaac stood at the top of the stairs, safe if a little pale.

Julia took in the scene, her eyes frantically darting from Eli to Carly…then to Ariel. She lunged toward the baby.

With all the strength left in her, Carly swung, her forearm catching Julia in the throat.

With a strangled cry, the other woman dropped to her knees.

Eli stepped into the room, his weapon aimed at Julia while the police officer rushed in and handcuffed her.

"Ariel." Carly could barely shove the word out. She reached for her goddaughter and lifted the screaming baby, holding her close and shaking, trying to calm the child while she felt like she was falling apart.

Low voices murmured and feet shuffled. When Ariel quieted and Carly looked up, only Eli was in the room.

He pulled her side close to his chest and bent his head low over Ariel. "It's really over now. Finished. You're both safe."

Sirens wailed in the distance, overlaid by the sounds of Julia shouting at the police officer as he led her down the stairs. "How did she find us?"

"OCPD doesn't typically keep a safe house, but they had an unusual circumstance with a protected witness briefly a few weeks ago. The DA's office set it all up, so she likely took a stab in the dark that they'd brought you here. Because no one knew she was involved, no one thought to keep her out of the loop. Even the cop on duty downstairs thought nothing of her coming in here."

As Ariel's cries quieted, Carly buried her face in Eli's neck. "I want to go home."

"I know." His arm tightened around her, and he pressed a kiss on her forehead. "And I'll make sure you get there as soon as the police take your statement."

"I'll go with her." Isaac spoke from behind her. While she wanted Eli, she understood his job, that he likely would have to stay here and deal with the aftermath of Julia's assault.

And after that?

After that she prayed with all of her heart that she could finally tell him the truth…that she wanted to build a life with him, if he was ready.

"I know you want to get back to Carly." Lizzie fell into step beside Eli as he left the briefing room, intent on grabbing Wrangler from his kennel and going straight to his car. "But I wanted to talk to you about something."

It was getting late, and he had an hour's drive ahead of him. "If you walk with me to get Wrangler, then we can talk. After that, I'm out the door." He had nothing on his agenda for the next two days, and he planned to use those two days to convince Carly that they needed to be together.

Emmett's briefing had been a mandatory face-to-face with the K-9 unit and the FBI, updating them on the case and handing out assignments based on new intel. It felt like they hadn't moved forward much, but they were all committed and driven.

Lizzie chuckled but didn't comment on his urgency. "So, Emmett left something out of the meeting, and I asked if I could pass the news along to you."

He almost stopped walking. If it was bad news, he wasn't sure he wanted to know. "Please tell me it's something hopeful."

"For once, yes. It's about Sarah Martin, the young pregnant women we saved from getting kidnapped outside the clinic."

He'd wondered about her, but given the chaos since her rescue, he hadn't been able to ask. "How's she doing?"

"Well, she said she can remember a handful of people showing interest in her over the past few weeks, asking questions she considered to be a bit intrusive, so likely there are a couple of operatives seeking out these women or they pay bystanders to ferret out intel for them."

"She'd said that at the clinic. Did we get anything from the security cameras in the store?"

"No." Lizzie's voice held thinly veiled disgust. "The cameras are old and the images are grainy, so the best you can tell is that they're people. No details."

Eli groaned as he shoved through the door into the kennel area. He'd been hoping…

But maybe with this new intel from Sarah, they could work toward prevention. How did they get the word out to young pregnant women that danger was lurking? He knew that the team had alerted some clinics in Denver, but Colorado was a big state and who knew how far the baby-smuggling ring's reach went? "Maybe we need to get with the pregnancy centers and get some flyers or texts pushed out to give these women a heads-up?"

"Eva's already working on it, but I have good news about Sarah. You know Dodger and his big heart." *And wallet*, was the unspoken rest of that comment. The man put his money where his mouth was when it came to causes he cared about. Even this training center had been funded by him. "One of the things he's been working on under the radar since Mia went missing is setting up a home for women like Sarah who have no one to turn to. She'll be one of the first residents. There will be room and board, access to medical care, and educational opportunities for the women so they don't become victims."

Eli breathed a sigh of relief. "That's awesome." At a time when they kept beating their heads against brick walls, it was nice to feel like something constructive was being done.

As he passed the training area, he slowed to watch their lead trainer, Dev Singh, working with one of their newest recruits, the German shepherd pup named Trooper.

Trooper's brother was excelling in training. Trooper, on the other hand, was proving to be a challenge, to say the least.

When Dev looked up, Eli cautiously skirted the issue of the K-9's temperaments. "How's it going?"

Dev commanded Trooper to sit and stay, then walked over to Lizzie and Eli.

The K-9 bounded around the room as though nothing had been said.

Lizzie winced. "Well, I see nothing's changed."

Raising both eyebrows in a silent *You think?* Dev looked back at the Shepherds. "I've been doing this for decades, and now, right as I want to retire, Trooper is determined to be the one K-9 I can't train. He's as sweet as can be, but..." He threw his hands into the air. "I just don't know."

"How's his brother?" Eli thought Trooper was a great dog, but as K-9 material, he was vexing everyone.

"Chance is excelling since I separated them. They love seeing each other at playtime, but Chance thrives on the work. Trooper thrives on the play." He turned and watched Trooper sniff the training area. "We're still working on finding my replacement. I think I might just make this a test for the top three candidates. The one who can train Trooper gets the job."

"You do want to retire, right?" Lizzie's voice held amusement.

"Don't even joke." Dev groaned, but he followed it with a grin. "Trooper may be an unsolvable problem, but he might make somebody a great pet. Maybe. If he could learn even the most basic of commands. He's smart, he's just not willing."

Lizzie elbowed him. "Be smart, Eli. Be willing."

Had she really just...? He rolled his eyes, but she was right. He was smart enough to know it was time to start living again.

And he was certainly willing.

It was getting dark when Eli parked the SUV, released Wrangler, and walked around his house to the paddock. He petted Sandy's neck and scratched Thunder's nose, spending an extra second with Hailey's horse. "What would you say if you knew what I was planning?"

"He'd say you're an idiot for being here instead of next door telling that girl how you feel about her."

It was a full second before he realized that the voice had

come from behind him and that it was Isaac, not the horses, who'd spoken. He was tired if he'd thought for an instant that Thunder had words for him. "Why aren't you with Carly?"

Isaac stepped up to the railing beside him and scratched Sandy behind the ear. "You accusing me of falling down on the job?" He smiled. "She's fine. She kicked me out. Wanted a shower and a few minutes to get the kid settled down in the crib. We got it all moved, by the way."

"Thank you. Really." He couldn't wait to hear Carly's reaction. He'd phoned in a few favors from members of OCPD and his church to move Ariel's nursery from Wendy's house into Carly's.

"I'm about to head back to the cabin." There was no emotion in Isaac's voice. He was stating a fact and wanted no argument.

Eli nodded. He'd known the older man wouldn't hang around for any longer than he had to. It was surprising he'd consented to a trip to the ER after Julia Crosby tasered him. With a clean bill of health, he was going back to where he was, if not happy, at least content.

With a slap on Eli's back, Isaac turned toward the house. "I'll come back in a couple of weeks. I'd like to see how much that kid grows in that time. I'm guessing a lot."

Eli's eyebrow arched. Count him double surprised. Ariel had sweetened the man's bitter heart.

"And Eli?"

He turned toward the house.

Isaac held the screened door open, eyeing Eli with a level gaze. "The horses are fine. You have no reason not to be at your neighbor's." He stepped up onto the porch. "Don't become an old fool like me." The screen door shut behind him. A minute later, the sound of Isaac's pickup disappeared into the distance.

He smiled. Joke was on Isaac. He had no intention of becoming an old fool.

Unless he became an old fool in love.

He wrinkled his forehead. That was sappy. Hailey would laugh if she could hear him.

Carly would, too.

He jogged across the yard and through the trees, reversing Carly's route from a few nights earlier. It was shorter than jogging up the road, and he wasn't about to waste a second. She'd had plenty of time to get Ariel settled in.

It was time for them to talk.

He slowed, not wanting to scare her by bursting into the yard, and because…

Was he certain he could do this? Was he prepared to embrace his memories while stepping into a new future? Once he said the words on his heart, he didn't want to take them back.

When he looked up, she was sitting on the porch, rocking gently and staring at the road. In denim shorts and a gray tee, she looked cool and comfortable. Her dark hair hung loose around her shoulders, stirring in the breeze from the ceiling fan. For the first time in days, she looked like she was at peace.

As she should be. Julia Crosby, Les Cassel and the others were behind bars, waiting for the justice system to move forward.

When Cassel had found out Julia was in custody, he'd confessed to working with her. He'd get the money, and she'd get Ariel.

When she'd gone off-script and killed Wendy, Cassel had panicked at her cruelty and had tried to accelerate their plan to appease her.

It had proven to be their downfall.

But it was all over now, and Ariel was safe. Carly was safe.

As he watched her rock on the porch, he knew…

He was also safe. He had loved Hailey with all he had in him, "until death do us part." He would always love her. He'd always love Ivy.

But that didn't mean his heart didn't have more love to give.

Was he sure?

He stepped out of the trees. Yes, he was sure.

At the motion, Carly stood and walked down the steps, a smile on her face when she met him halfway. "I figured you'd come up the road, not sneak through the woods."

He bit back a smile. He hadn't told her he was coming over, but she'd known…because she knew him.

He took in the sight of her. A baby monitor hung on a clip from her pocket. He'd rarely seen her hair down and, as it turned out, he liked it. A lot. He cleared his throat. "Where's Ariel?"

"Asleep in a crib that somehow made its way from Wendy's house to mine while I was giving my statement at the police station. Would you happen to know who did that?" Her head cocked adorably to one side.

"Maybe."

She stepped closer, closing the space between them. "I should say thank you…if the person who orchestrated that is ready to hear it."

His heart took up an extra beat. It was an invitation to tell her what he wanted. She wouldn't force her way into his life, but she'd listen to whatever he had to say whenever he was ready to say it.

Once again, he was ready.

He scanned her eyes, her hair, her lips…

"What are you looking at?" Her voice was a whisper, as

though she was scared he might bolt like a frightened horse if she made too much noise.

"You." He closed the gap between them and ran his finger gently down her cheek. "The future." His finger paused at her lower lip. "Me, you, Ariel…a family. If that's what you want."

Her lips parted into a slow smile. She grabbed his hand, pulled it to her waist, then leaned in and kissed him, softly at first, then fiercely, as though she'd been waiting for this moment her whole life.

It was likely she had.

And maybe he had, too.

* * * * *

If you enjoyed this story,
don't miss Fugitive Manhunt,
the next book in the
Colorado K-9 Unit series!
Discover all the books in this brand-new continuity:

Searching for the Truth *by Laura Scott*
Tracking the Taken Child *by Sharon Dunn*
Danger in the Rockies *by Terri Reed*
Protecting the Baby *by Jodie Bailey*
Fugitive Manhunt *by Sharee Stover*
Hunting an Arsonist *by Jessica R. Patch*
Uncovering Explosive Secrets *by Maggie K. Black*
Unraveling a Crime Ring *by Valerie Hansen*
Christmas K-9 Security *by Lynette Eason & Lenora Worth*

Available only from Love Inspired Suspense!

Dear Reader,

In 2017, one of our sister churches lost their pastor in an accident. Two young children lost their dad. A wife lost her husband.

A couple years later, I attended a women's event where his wife spoke. She talked about her love for her husband and the terrible grief that had consumed her family. But then she said something incredible. She said, "Though he was a wonderful part of my life, he was not my *entire* life." As a woman who dearly loves her husband, that struck me to the core. I still think about it. Her time with her husband had been one of the most beautiful chapters of her life, a treasure she could have never dreamed. His story had ended. Hers had not. God had her here to touch others and to keep moving, even though grief was so heavy some days.

Eli's story was tough to write, because grief and healing are personal things that we all experience differently. The *why* can be so confusing. I don't have easy answers. I wish I did. Grief makes us angry and sad and confused and a thousand other emotions we wish we never had to feel. Worse, it never truly goes away.

I do believe with all my heart—and I promise these aren't just words—that God is near to those whose hearts are broken (Psalm 34:18) and that someday He will wipe every tear from our eyes and there will be no more sadness or death (Revelation 21:4). I really do look forward to that day, and I pray you do, too.

For those who are hurting, I'm praying for you. You're on my heart.

Jodie Bailey

Get up to 4 Free Books!

We'll send you 2 free books from each series you try
PLUS a free Mystery Gift.

Both the **Love Inspired**® and **Love Inspired**® **Suspense** series feature compelling novels filled with inspirational romance, faith, forgiveness and hope.

YES! Please send me 2 FREE novels from the Love Inspired or Love Inspired Suspense series and my FREE gift (gift is worth about $10 retail). I may cancel anytime by emailing ReaderServiceInfo@Harlequin.com or by calling 1-800-873-8635. If I don't cancel, I will receive 6 brand-new Love Inspired Larger-Print books or Love Inspired Suspense Larger-Print books every month and be billed just $7.19 each in the U.S. or $7.99 each in Canada. That is a savings of 20% off the cover price. It's quite a bargain! Shipping and handling is just 75¢ per book in the U.S. and $1.75 per book in Canada.* I understand that accepting the free books and gift places me under no obligation to buy anything—they are mine to keep for free no matter what I decide.

Choose one:
- ☐ **Love Inspired Larger-Print** (122/322 BPA G3CD)
- ☐ **Love Inspired Suspense Larger-Print** (107/307 BPA G3CD)
- ☐ **Or Try Both!** (122/322 & 107/307 BPA G3CE)

Name (please print)

Address   Apt. #

City   State/Province   Zip/Postal Code

Email: Please check this box ☐ if you would like to receive newsletters and promotional emails from Harlequin Enterprises ULC and its affiliates. You can unsubscribe anytime.

Mail to the Harlequin Reader Service:
IN U.S.A.: P.O. Box 1341, Buffalo, NY 14240-8531
IN CANADA: P.O. Box 603, Fort Erie, Ontario L2A 5X3

Want to explore our other series or interested in ebooks? Visit www.ReaderService.com or call 1-800-873-8635.

LIRLIS2603